CRY LEBANON

'Just come. *Please*, Lois. Come quickly. We need you here!'

If it's your sister calling, and she's ringing you from Beirut, you go. In the crippled and lawless city a hit has gone wrong, leaving a young girl dead. This demands vengeance, the taking of hostages, an eye for an eye. Two political groups, equally ruthless, confront each other, jockeying for position, seeking to get in the next blow. Nothing is certain; no one, however close to you, can be trusted. It is a terrifying experience – one that, if you survive it, marks you for life. Lois Everard has seen it all before, but has never been directly involved ... until now.

This is a tense and moving novel of Beirut during a relatively 'quiet' period.

CRY LEBANON

JANE MORELL

ROBERT HALE · LONDON

ISBN 0 7090 4055 5

Robert Hale Limited
Clerkenwell House
Clerkenwell Green
London EC1R 0HT

Photoset in North Wales by
Derek Doyle & Associates, Mold, Clwyd.
Printed in Great Britain by
St Edmundsbury Press, Bury St Edmunds, Suffolk.
Bound by WBC Bookbinders Limited.

To GEORGETTE,
and many others, there

May God guard the vineyard from its watchmen
Lebanese proverb

One

The city spreads wide round the harbour and from it broad roads sweep inland to the cradling hills. Breaking smoothly against the shores of the curving coast, the sea promises rich fishing. The air is full of morning sunshine, spring-warm.

But the name of the city is Beirut: the sea here is dying from pollution; the sunshine is always tired, always hazed with the fine dust drifting from the thousands of shell-struck buildings that are crumbling away year by year into total ruin; and the broken pavements smell of past and present violence, and of death.

The people of the city no longer notice these things: they are part of today's living so get on with it, live your own life – and hope your own death isn't waiting for you round the next corner, in the barrel of someone's gun or in the red heart of the grenade gripped in the hand of that arm already arched to throw –

Carefully, Ramadan Saad placed the mango in his hand on its prepared bed of green leaves, together with the five others already displayed there, well to the forefront of his fruit-stall. Stood back to consider the effect of the whole, then: cool and tempting in the shade of an old almond-tree, apples, strawberries, peaches, oranges, grapefruit – and these gorgeous mangoes flown in from Egypt, rich yellow shading to a rosy ripeness ... So; nothing to do now but wait for customers ...

Wiping his hands on the towel tucked into his belt, he took a few steps forward to stand at the crossroads where 'his' road, the side-street Rue 27 where the Group allowed him his pitch, was intersected by Bokdassi, the main shopping street of this area of West Beirut. A wiry dark-skinned man in his thirties, he walked with a slight limp, his right knee unable to bear his full weight, his right foot fitted with a special boot. To those who hadn't known him before the fighting of '75 he says he has been crippled since birth; but the people who really matter to him (most of whom are, like himself, members of Abu Hamad's section of the pro-Iran FFP Group) know the date of the day during whose nightmare hours he acquired his limp and they know how and why that happened: old history now, but it is why the FFP awarded him his pitch in the first place and – since some acts live forever in men's minds – is why now, fifteen years later, that Group keeps any rival claimants to it at bay by the usual method, intimidation (of proven ferocity, in this case).

At the crossroads, Saad settled his weight on his left foot and leg, looked up and then down Bokdassi. After a moment, heard the bleeper on his watch sound the hour and thought idly: ten o'clock, I wonder if Abu Hamad will be passing here this morning, he often does around this time on Tuesdays ... Not much traffic. Not many people about yet, either ... Along there on the right, where all the cars are parked, Mindani's department store, useful shop, that, not too pricey and value for money ... Wonder if I dare put those mangoes at 25? Better maybe put them at 23 and get rid of them while they're still worth it ...

Suddenly he caught sight in the distance of a black Mercedes approaching the crossroads, heading downtown along Bokdassi ... Nearer, and it was surely Abu Hamad's but there was no 'lead' car travelling ahead of it, pacing it (and carrying the heavily armed bodyguards) so the big man of FFP wasn't in it himself today ... Side- and rear-window blinds down, though, so likely to be someone inside, some high-up of the Group, maybe, or a known hit-man on business ...

The Mercedes slid by, gleaming, travelling at a steady 50 kph; and Saad dismissed from his mind 'the old days' when 'Abu Hamad' had been simply Mouchtar Hajj, friend and comrade of Ramadan Saad, the two young men of an age and already making a name for themselves within the FFP for dare-devil courage and an arrogant skill with guns ... Turning away, he limped back towards his stall; he had a stool there and it would be good to sit down for a bit, he'd been up at four a.m., down at the market ...

Other eyes had been watching for the approach of the Mercedes.

Standing apparently motiveless on the top step of the four leading up to the triple-doored entrance to Mindani's store, 200 yards beyond Saad's crossroads, the elderly man smoking a cigarette spotted the black car just as Saad turned away: and straightening, took the cigarette from his mouth, dropped it at his feet and ground it out with the toe of his scuffed brown shoe; then settled his brown hat more firmly on his head and walked down the steps and away along the pavement. All these actions unhurried: a man with time to spare (his part already played).

Not so for those who are working with him and now act on his signal. Two of them there are, both positioned inside the store at carefully chosen points of vantage to keep the old man well in view: young men, these, dressed student-casual in denim caps, jeans and sneakers, hands thrust deep into the pockets of their windcheaters. The one nearer the door, the 'blocker' of the imminent operation, moves out first, pushing open one of the glass doors with his left hand, the right still clenched in his pocket. The second – he is twenty-four years old, his *nom de guerre* is Shawki and he is a hard and intelligent young man, very ambitious in this his chosen profession – goes out of Mindani's two seconds later, stands aside most politely holding his door open for a smartly-dressed woman (who walks past him, into the store, with a quiet 'Merci') then moves on down the steps and into the spring sunshine of Bokdassi Street.

Street morning-quiet, office- and shop-workers already 9 to 2 imprisoned, most shoppers-to-be still at home doing the chores. Shawki sees the black Mercedes approaching him; it is no more than 50 yards from him and already his 'blocker' is moving in for the kill – *but there is no lead car!* For a split second Shawki's mind swings wild, off balance because if Abu Hamad's in the Merc there should be a 'lead' car *and there isn't one* – then training asserts its discipline.

Shit! Get on with it man! *'Once the plan is activated, follow it through whatever happens.'* So quit speculating and get to work.

The Mercedes glides towards him, the face of its driver a mask seen through glass; off to his right he sees/senses the blocker's arm swing high over his head, then sunlight goes out in a blast of dust and flame and flying debris and the street-and-people-living sounds are engulfed in one tremendous echoing bang as the grenade explodes in the roadway, close in under the bonnet of the Mercedes.

Keeping his distance, Shawki draws his RV2C Special and shoots in the nearside front window of the Merc – he fires four times – then switches the weapon to his left hand. Pulls his grenade from the pocket of his windcheater: this, though smaller than the other, the 'ensuring' agent. Priming it, hurls it sidearm through the smashed-out window, into the interior of the car. But his aim is faulty (though he does not know it): in its flight the grenade strikes a front seat head-rest, and bounces *down*, coming to rest at the driver's feet. Explodes *then* –

As he turns to run his eyes sweep over the scene, searching out importances: the driver's sprawled half out of the wreck, he's dead, there isn't enough of him left for him to be alive; the Merc hasn't caught fire, yet; the blocker's already out of sight –

And Shawki is running. The people nearest to him seem turned to stone but he is running *and not one of them is looking at him*: some are flat on the pavement, arms covering their heads, others cower in doorways, flinching away as he passes – then he sees, ahead of him, pressing herself back against the wall on the corner where he'll turn left, a young girl. She's sixteen/ seventeen years old and she's dressed in school uniform, blue skirt white blouse with a bright red tie – odd to notice that when I'm on the run with all hell screaming behind me, but all the time I'm getting closer to her and she's staring straight at me and *she doesn't look away*; her hat's down on the pavement, long dark hair, face yellowy pale, shock, eyes brown *staring into my face*. Look away girl, this is killer, wisest never to see the face of a killer, most people know that by this time but I see you've still got a lot of learning to do –

He draws level with her. Still she stares at his face. Then for an instant Shawki finds his eyes caught and held by hers and some deep indefinable knowledge flashes between him and the girl; he feels, as if it were his own, the blood-and-bone terror in her, but also the concentrated will holding it at bay; senses her hatred streaming at him and realizes she is engaged in searing the very elements of his face and being into her memory *so that she will never forget either*.

Momentarily, he falters, conscious suddenly of feeling cold (the girl perceives a sort of tiredness, a loss of élan, loosen his face). Then he drags his eyes free of hers and picks up speed, turns the corner into the haven of Rue 23 and stops running. Walks on, steadily. After a while, laughs to himself. Not a damn one of those people back there will ever come forward as witness against the slayer of Abu Hamad, he says to himself. They have learnt by now, our citizens. The men on top can get a load of teaching done in fifteen years …

But when he remembers the girl, Shawki was not nearly so sure – of several things.

Ramadan Saad and two other men had pulled all movable wreckage away from the driver of the Mercedes and his two passengers by the time the rescue services arrived and ambulance- and firemen took over. The three of them stood back then, watched briefly.

'A miracle the boy survived,' observed the businessman, dusting off his crumpled suit. 'Got himself down on the floor in time.'

'His sister, not so lucky.' Saad frowning, preoccupied.

'You know them?' Surprised, the third man – a

cashier from a nearby bank – turned to look at the slim
dark man with the limp and the unexpected strength
just put to such good use.

'Sure. They were brother and sister. Chap in front
was the chauffeur … It won't stop here, this killing,' he
went on sombrely. 'There'll be trouble from it –' But he
broke off, becoming aware that the other two were
regarding him now with a sudden coldness – perhaps
suspicion? Certainly there was hostility – well, no great
wonder in that, they'd know the attack was a terrorist hit
of some kind and usually the ordinary citizen preferred
to keep himself well clear of incidents of that nature;
once get drawn into the vengeance syndrome and you
could only too easily be the next on someone's list …
Abruptly, Saad voiced a curt farewell and turned away:
sure of his own allegiances, born and bred to them, he
had only contempt for those who refused to take sides
in the one, the vital struggle.

As he limped back to his stall he wiped sweat and
grime from his face and hands; and eyed the sunlit
street grimly. Inevitably, *big* trouble would flow from
the strike just carried out. Bungled, it had been, too, for
'they' – whoever they might be – had surely been after
Abu Hamad himself. Instead, they had 'got' his two
children. Someone would pay for that, by God! And
Abu Hamad wasn't the type to bother with the paid help
who'd actually thrown the grenades; he'd go after *the
boss-man who had given the orders for the strike against him,
the man with the executive power to organize that* …

Hessa, lying dead in her blood back there: bullet
through the right eye even before the grenade. Hessa,
Abu Hamad's daughter, aged fifteen; the year she was
born Hamad and me level-pegging in the Group, plenty
action then and I got my leg shot up … *Hessa, dead now.*

Praise be to God that Imad survived it, saved by the armoured seat in front of him. Abu Hamad's only son, eleven years old, lively youngster and 'into' football these days ... No football for a while yet, boy, maybe never again, those injuries looked pretty bad ...

Graced by the patterned shade of the almond-tree, the fruit-stall was full of colour, inviting the eye. Saad did good business that morning, the excellence of his produce compensation enough to his customers for his unwonted taciturnity. He found it difficult to give himself to the trivia of trading that day; there was an urge in him to shout out to the city around him, '*Watch out!* Hessa is dead by terror-strike and her father's name is Abu Hamad!' That would be warning enough, for it was well known – by the blood-and-fire experience of many, not only by hearsay – that behind the pseudonym existed a man who held to a ruthless code of vengeance and who had at his command the men and the resources to implement the dictates of that code.

Saad left his pitch at 2.30, as usual. But already a messenger had come to him requesting that he report to Abu Hamad that evening. He had expected the summons; would obey it; and was already impatient for the meeting. Was eager to move again in the ambience of the brotherhood within which Abu Hamad had attained such high position; and therein to feel himself once more part of one of the powers in the land. Blood for blood: an ancient and satisfying creed ...

Two

' ...And if I'm not in by midday tomorrow, you take young Airey to lunch. My apologies and so on; influenza, I should suggest.' Roberts smiled up at her across his desk. 'A lot of it about, I believe.'

Lois Everard smiled back without enthusiasm: she found Michael Airey an irritatingly self-pleased young man; but his last novel had done remarkably well and the readers' reports on his new one all indicated that it would be a wise move for 'Falcon Press', as a relatively new and independent publishing house very much on the look-out for fresh talent, to accept it for publication.

'Were I of a vindictive nature I should light candles to ensure that you did indeed fall victim,' she said (such acidities being permitted since she had been with Roberts since he started the company four years ago and was now his secretary; no, more, she was his aide-de-camp). 'However –'

'Ferguson still in Hong Kong?' He was watching her as she walked away towards the door: she had a young and beautiful body and he enjoyed her physical presence, as always, but there was no lust in his awareness of her, at sixty he was still happily married to the girl he had fallen in love with during his last year at college.

She halted, turning to face him. 'Yes. He's due back in ten days' time.'

'You miss him.' Statement, not question; he knew that Dan Ferguson and she had been lovers for the last eight months, and assumed them headed for eventual marriage.

Now, she smiled again – then wiped the smile from her face, and frowned. 'The more I enjoy my work here, the less I miss him, I find,' she said. 'His job takes him abroad such a lot, I've had time to learn that.'

'Sublimation?' He offered it, tentatively, holding her eyes.

She shook her head. 'You can fall in love, so presumably you can fall out of it.' Abruptly, she swung away. 'Booker Prize for tritest observation of year,' she suggested, and left the room swiftly …

Ten minutes later, work tidied up for the day and office farewells made, Lois stepped out into Lewes High Street. The day was cool and windy, and she pulled up the collar of her coat and set off briskly for home: a fifteen-minute walk, mostly uphill. Of medium height, with a trim waist and good legs, she strode along zestfully, auburn shoulder-length hair blowing in the wind and she loving the freshness of it, lifting her face to it. Briefly, she thought about Dan Ferguson: admitting she missed him physically, oh yes, the body crying for him, fiercely desiring him; but – was she indeed learning to live quite happily with his frequent absences? And if so, what of the future –

Forget him now, said the wind in her hair. So she did. And with the ease of the forgetting making both a sadness and a joy in her, let herself into her ground-floor flat in the big house at the top of the hill; and after making a pot of tea and drinking it, changed

into a tracksuit and wellingtons and spent an hour
working in the garden at the back, lilacs in bloom, roses
in leaf – and weeds rioting behind the summer-house,
pretty, some of them, but harden your heart (selectively,
the brilliance of a bank of speedwell in full flower
causing the idea of 'tidiness' to wither instantly) ...

The telephone rang just after seven o'clock. She went
into the living-room from the kitchen, apron still on.

Person-to-person call, said the operator; from Beirut.
So she knew: not Dan, but her sister Tagarid – *or some
official stranger calling to inform her that Tagarid was dead?*
This, the imagined horror lurking behind every call
from Beirut she took and never dispelled until she
heard her sister's voice saying her usual quiet 'Is that
you, Lois?'

As it did now, thank God. All well, then – but was it?
The voice – Tagarid's, yes, but a strange, clipped quality
to it –?

'Tagarid. are you all right?' But a thin hissing on the
line, blurred words half-surfacing then submerged
beneath it. 'Tell me –!'

'Lois?' Suddenly, the line clear. 'Listen. I may lose you
any moment so please, just *listen*. I want you to come out
here. As soon as you can. I *need* you –'

'You're safe?' The fear Lois lives with; and now gets
no answer to quieten.

'Never mind! There isn't time! We may get cut off any
second.' (True indeed: Lois knows it and holds back her
own words to leave room for those of her sister.) 'Please,
come as soon as you can. *We need you* –'

'But my job! I can't just drop everything unless – Tell
me *why*, Tagarid! What's wrong out there?'

The hissing rushed in again, louder, and she held the
receiver away from her ear waiting for it to clear as it

had done before. Suddenly it lessened; but still it lived, and when she held the receiver close to listen again she heard it like a rough sea breaking on shingle and her sister's voice coming through faint but still the toneless quality to it.

'Just – *come*. I'll tell you everything when you're here. *Please*, Lois. Come quickly. We need you *here!*'

A loud crackling, then the line went dead. No Tagarid; not even that hissing 'sea' out of which her voice might come again … When to wait longer became pointless Lois replaced the receiver, went across to the window-seat, sat down on its green cushions and stared out at the garden. But saw no lilacs …

'We need you.' '*We*'. That has to mean all three of them: Tagarid, Soheil, Liliane.

Tagarid the beautiful. Me, Lois, I'm pretty good to look at, too; but my sister is beautiful. Also, she is sophisticated and truly elegant. Even before she married Soheil, she was all those things; and since she married him six years ago, the *quality* of all those attributes has become somehow richer. Through their loving? Yes, I imagine because of that: before her marriage there had always been a sort of coldness to her, a sort of withdrawal of herself from closeness to other people. Including me. That 'wall' of Tagarid's self-sufficiency against which I used to batter away with all my hot-blooded urgency to get 'close' to her – Soheil reached out his hand and touched that wall and it simply melted away …

Soheil. The man known to me, except for the physical reality of him, mostly through Tagarid's words, letters. That physical reality perceived during my last five visits to Beirut; once a year, and each for a month … A tallish man, he's only a couple of inches taller than she, quite narrowly built but a muscular strength to him; good eyes, yes, therein lies the secret of Soheil's immediate impact upon others ... And, of course, there's his 'gift'. His undoubted, wonderful and highly prized 'gift': he is a superb eye-surgeon. Soheil's 'other two loves', as Tagarid calls them: his work, and – the Lebanon. Many offers he's received, from the States, from Japan, but he'll have none of them until Lebanon is at peace within itself, and prospering again ...

And Liliane. Sixteen, now. The girl they adopted three years ago when her parents were killed during a random shelling in the city, direct hit on their house – their shack, Tagarid termed it, for they were poor. Tagarid coming into the situation through her work with Save The Children: many similar cases, of course, but – to her – Liliane different, special in some way. It happens ... And now the girl like a daughter ...

The garden spread out before her eyes was suddenly lit with sunshine and she *saw* it. Came back with a slight shock of surprise – disbelief, almost – to her flat, to Lewes, England. Looking out at her flowering lilacs, heard her sister's words again and felt fear close in around her because *they came from Beirut*.

'I want you to come out here.' Tagarid's voice but – under terrible strain.

'Please, come as soon as you can.' Tagarid *pleading* with me.

'*We need you here.*'

Lois got to her feet and went to the telephone. When you get a call like that *from a place like that*, you go. Oh yes, you go. Fast ...

Zahlé is a town famous for its cherries. Flanking the main road that runs from Beirut to Shtaura then close in

under the Lebanon mountains and along the broad and
fertile Beka'a Valley, to Baalbek – then on to Damascus
– it was the scene of much bloody strife between
Christian and Muslim during the early '80s; and now
'enjoys' relative peace – and the presence of the Syrian
army. The cherry-trees flower and fruit as bountifully
as ever under this 'occupation'. The townsfolk, Muslim
and Christian alike, (though there are fewer of the latter
nowadays), go about the ordinary affairs of their living.
Some of them – of both religions – are engaged in
clandestine political activities, and these move very
carefully indeed before their fellow-men, remembering
certain months in '81 which, for a few, are and always
will be totally unforgettable, powering their present
stratagems and informing them with the necessary
hatred.

One such was the man whose code-name within his
cadre was 'Othman'. A Muslim farmer who loved his
land and worked it well, he loathed all Christians: a
violent hatred braided into the fibre of his being during
the fighting of ten years ago when his father and his two
brothers had been killed in a Muslim-to-Christian
hand-to-hand battle on the outskirts of the town.
Othman had survived: thereafter to cherish only his
land – and his bitterness. And seeking to assuage the
hatred in him, had become a member of the pro-Syrian
Group known as the FFP – pro-Syrian being *de facto*
anti-Christian, which was the only thing that mattered
to him – and on instructions from its Beirut-based
Command had brought into being a four-man local
band-of-brothers of like mind with himself. Zahlé being
well stocked with Syrian troops, the work he had done
to date had been small stuff – Central Command in
Beirut had assured him it was all extremely useful, true,

but there had been nothing to satisfy his own craving for (if possible) enemy blood.

Nothing big – until the previous day, 6th May. Yesterday morning, just: the word-of-mouth instruction from Command HQ, Beirut, delivered by the usual truck-driver in as workaday fashion as always – but the orders themselves not workaday. In the name of God, not that. Action: at last, *action!*

Now, in the prepared hide-out deep in the hills behind Zahlé – a long-deserted farmhouse in the lee of a copse of conifers, with strategic lookout positions commanding the track leading in along the valley floor – Othman recalled the words of that directive. 'Seize two hostages from AKAL. Take to safe hide. Forward to this office ID details of men seized. Hold prisoners and await further instructions. Action immediate. Repeat immediate.'

Othman turned up the wick of the hurricane-lamp on the rough wooden table he was sitting at, leaned back in his camp chair; and a smile of grim satisfaction lengthened his lips. The hostages had been taken as ordered: a well-planned raid on Said Abdullah's isolated barn outside Zahlé, the shack where he and such of his godless fellow-AKAL supporters as felt so inclined met every Saturday during the period of afternoon rest. Four of them had turned up there today – no guards, the fools, supposing themselves secure because they always kept a low profile, never actually made any move against the occupying force – so he and his men had simply busted in, selected a couple of them (the two not known to them by sight; best to keep your face covered and steer clear of 'locals' if possible or you might suffer some 'wild justice' yourself later on!), knocked out and tied up the others. Then, had herded the two captives into the Datsun van and taken off for the hills ...

Now it was time to get down to further business: IDs and so on. The prospect of interrogating his captives intrigued Othman, fuelling a certain pride in him: he was (albeit temporarily) *master* of these two AKAL bastards!

'Guard!' he shouted. And when the man came in from his station outside the door, ordered that the prisoner be brought before him.

'Which one?'

'The city man. The other's a peasant, I shan't bother with him myself. You get his papers from him, bring them to me later.'

The guard brought in the 'city man', stood him in front of the table, then withdrew, closing the door behind him.

Captor eyed captive. Saw: a man in his thirties; slim, yes, but he held himself well and beneath the black suede jacket his shoulders were good, not meaty but he looked like a man accustomed to use his body, no 'clerkly stoop' to him ... Clean-shaven, straight dark hair – *and the eyes*. As he met the concentrated gaze of his prisoner, Othman felt himself suddenly somehow smaller. Diminished. Physically, yes, but deep inside himself, too. A weird, disquieting uncertainty – gone in a heartbeat as he brought his own will to bear and refused to look away. Then the 'other' eyes let up their pressure; and smiled into his own.

'Sit down,' Othman said. And knew he had spoken to break – the silence, perhaps?

Captive eyed captor. Saw: a burly man in a checkered shirt; black-bearded, strong-growing black hair. In his weathered square-jawed face the mouth narrow-lipped, the eyes small and quick: a moody and possibly vicious man, this – but faltering now, the macho image (self-image?) not standing up under challenge.

'Will you untie my hands for a while?' His voice quiet. 'The cord is tight and they have been tied for five hours now. My hands are important to me.' Again the brown eyes smiled. 'Important to others, also,' he added.

'How so?'

'My work. I am an eye-surgeon.'

Retreating into a suspicious silence, Othman considered the request. At last, got to his feet; and drawing a clasp-knife from his pocket, stepped round the table and cut through the cords binding the prisoner's wrists.

'Put your papers on the table,' he ordered (immediately reasserting his authority as boss).

The 'city man' placed his leather wallet on the scarred wooden surface; and then sat down on the grubby broken-backed chair already in position on his side of the table.

Othman returned to his own place. Picking up the wallet he extracted from it several papers, glanced through them and finally spread open before him the two that interested him. Having studied these, raised his eyes once more to the man opposite him.

'Soheil Fanous. Lebanese. Employed at the American Hospital. Doctor. Specialist, surgery to the eyes.' He stated the facts he had gained from the papers aggressively, aiming to cover up the fact that he was impressed by the status of his prisoner.

'All true.' Fanous sat relaxed, his fingers massaging his wrists where the ropes had chafed them but his eyes fixed on the man facing him. 'Why have you abducted me?' he asked flatly.

Othman refused to be intimidated; but nevertheless, found himself answering. 'On orders,' he said. Then, angrily, '*I* question, not you!'

'Then ask your questions. You have made an error, I think, in taking me. I am a doctor. I have no part in politics.' During the hours since his abduction, Fanous had considered with great care the way he should 'play' this totally unexpected situation; had decided on the frank approach and a readiness to talk – and had driven home to his fellow-prisoner the need to stick to the 'cover' story already agreed between them.

Othman recalled that, actually, he had not been empowered to interrogate his captives. But he found himself interested in this man, even drawn to him; and in his (relative) simplicity had always held doctors of any sort in high regard.

'As I said, I am acting under orders,' he said pacifically. 'But I find it strange,' he went on, glancing across the table into the brilliant brown eyes and then quickly looking away, 'that a *doctor* should attend a meeting of AKAL supporters.' He gave a mirthless chuckle. 'No-one whose brain isn't addled could maintain that AKAL is not a political organization?'

'I was there to deliver messages and money to the man you brought in with me, Abbas Suleiman. His son works at the hospital and sends money home – he is a porter there – and I quite often meet Suleiman as I did today and for the same purpose.'

'Is there no postal service, then, from Beirut to Zahlé?' Sarcasm.

'Would *you* entrust *your* money to it?'

Othman laughed. Then sobering, took up another point. 'You say you have no part in politics,' he observed. Then leaned forward across the table and sought the other man's eyes; stared into them: his face hardened (and suddenly Fanous saw him as being, after all, a truly meaningful man). 'At this time, in Lebanon,' he went on harshly, 'no man who belongs here has a right to stand aside from the political battles that are being fought out. A man has a duty to make his choice, and then to stand by it to the death – his own death, or that of his foeman.' (An archaic word he used, Fanous noted; and liked him for it.)

'That is *your* stand?'

'I support the FFP. To the death.'

Fanous exerted his will, controlling both himself and his words (keep to one truth and voice it, with suitable slantings and deletions, and you may deceive your enemy – or indeed, your friend, when that is necessary).

'I see from your words that you know how it feels to be dedicated,' he said. 'So you should understand that a man cannot properly dedicate himself to two causes. I devote myself to my work. There is no room in my life for politics. My work uses up all of myself.'

Othman searched his eyes for a moment longer; then sat back, looking down at the knife-scored wood of the table. 'I believe you,' he said after a pause, a dull ache in him as – for a second only – he measured this man's commitment to the constructive and healing service of others against his own destructive, *known*-to-be destructive, *seeking*-to-be destructive ethos.

'What were you ordered to do with us?' Fanous edged the verb slightly, seeking to maintain the personal dominance he had, he believed, established over his captor – a minion, of course he was only that, but he was the one at the moment possessed of knowledge that might be of some use.

Othman shrugged: thinking to himself that he must

call in the guard, must get the prisoner tied up again and returned to rejoin his fellow in the outhouse; hoping that those 'further instructions' he had been told to await would come soon, and this doctor be taken off his hands. But (again) he found himself answering:

'Get your papers and forward them to Central Command. Keep the two of you secure while awaiting further orders.'

'You did not abduct us – myself and Suleiman – specifically?'

'Two AKAL hostages, that was the stipulation. And as it has been known to me for a long time that certain accursed AKAL men meet at that barn, engaging in their poisonous intrigues, I decided to raid it, take from there two men. Any two, of those there.'

'So why was *I* one of those seized? Others were present.'

A pause; then Othman looked up and in the yellow light of the lamp his eyes gleamed, a closed smile licked his lips briefly. 'Two reasons. The first, that I did not know you by sight or by repute and you did not know me, either. The second, that you looked to be the most important man there: far better dressed – other things about you, too. And important men are more useful as hostages.' He got to his feet and moved towards the door, shouting for the guard.

'These "further orders", when they arrive from your Central Command, may call for the execution of myself – of both myself and Suleiman.' Fanous spoke quietly, sitting unmoving in his chair, the fury inside him held in iron control.

Othman turned back to look at him, stood still, frowning; and realized that he hoped he would not have to kill this man, this surgeon, Soheil Fanous. It was a realization that greatly surprised him; and left him strangely uneasy, as though the wall of his moral self-confidence and certainty had been ever so slightly breached. A needle-thin puncture; but *it was there*. Nevertheless:

'Whatever I am instructed to do will be done,' he said, evenly.

Three

Sunlight is cruel to the ravaged city. It slides in beneath masks to reveal the hopelessness infesting people's faces; lays bare the bones of ruptured shops and offices; reaches into the hollow blackened shells of places where – once upon a time – men, women and children lived; shines in through broken windows to expose chaos and filth where – once upon a time – order and cleanliness reigned; and everywhere causes the dust born of bomb-blast and mortar fire and dead men's bones to glint and glitter, coming alive and shouting loudly of past agonies ...

Lois Everard looked out through the window of the taxi she had taken at Beirut airport and hated the sunlight for its brilliant exposure of the truth. A year gone by since her last visit; but the city and its people still engaged in their dreadful sporadic battles, no time no money *no heart* left for rebuilding (you surely need all you've got of the last to keep you going at all) ...

Withdrawing her gaze, she sat back, closing her eyes, forcing herself to relax. She had telephoned the apartment, from the airport, to make sure there was someone at home. 'Take a taxi,' Tagarid had said. 'I meant to be there to meet you, but ...' No reason had followed, only silence. Then: 'I'll be in', and the call

terminated. Uptight, Tagarid had sounded, even more
so than during that first call through to Lewes –

Lewes? Lois' eyes jerked open and she peered out
through the window again and at once the remembered
well-maintained freshness of Lewes fled to a far
country …

Shams House: the four-storey apartment block was
situated in a side-street near the curving thoroughfare
named Caracole el Druze, an imposing building of
faced yellow stone, each of its four apartments
occupying one entire floor. The taxi drew up alongside
the broken kerbing outside it. Lois paid off the driver,
got out, took her two suitcases one in either hand and
made her way across cracked and uneven pavement to
the courtyard: from there on the going was good (paid
for by the residents, even the absentee ones sending
cash from their foreign safe-havens to ensure the
proper upkeep of their properties). Smooth tiling led
into the spacious hall graced with massy green-gleaming
houseplants; the carpeted lift came when summoned
and then glided upwards to stop at the fourth floor, as
programmed.

Lois stepped out onto the landing of red polished
tiles, put her cases down outside the teak door of the
apartment – the flexed steel gates that were rolled
across at night and padlocked into position were left
open during the day – and rang the house-bell.

Nothing happened. Frowning, she waited, glancing
around her: to the right, the tiled stairway connecting
the floors; to her left, close to the lift-shaft, the concrete
steps leading up to the flat roof of the block, used by the
servants for the drying of laundry. Blown sand lay on
the steps, two out of the four flats empty, their owners
fled to Cyprus, and the third, the one on the ground

floor, lived in by its caretaker only ... As she reached out to ring for the second time, the door in front of her opened.

Tagarid. No make-up at all; the brown eyes beneath their slanted brows enormous and – dulled; mouth tight-lipped; black hair hanging loose and in need of brushing.

'Come in,' she said, picking up one of the cases, and the two sisters bundled their way in, put the cases down in the hall.

'Tagarid, now please –?'

'They've taken Soheil.' She closed the door; swung round. 'This Saturday, he was up at Zahlé on a regular visit and –'

'What d'you mean, "taken"? Kidnapped?'

'I don't *know*. I'm not sure.' She paused; her chin went up and she took a deep breath. Then went on, quietly now: 'Put your bags in your usual room and go into the lounge. I'll get some coffee. Tell you, then.'

Soheil Fanous stretched his legs out on the concrete floor and leaned his bruised back against the breeze-block wall of the room he and Suleiman had been locked into a short while ago. A dark place it was, one tiny window, and that set high up and grimed over with dirt. No furniture except two wooden beds and the bucket in the corner.

He had no idea where he was now. Sometime that morning – the first morning after the abduction, he reminded himself, no watch now and it helps orientation to keep track of the passage of time, if you can – the toughs who had abducted them had come into that first cell they'd been in, fairly close to Zahlé that one must have been, had gagged and blindfolded them and pushed them into the back of a truck of some kind. Then, had driven them around. For several hours, with three or four times a break during which the men up front got out and walked about – probably had some food, water – but the two captives in the back left shut up in their fetid darkness ... Most of the roads they'd travelled over had been extremely rough, and with their arms tied behind them and their eyes bandaged he and Suleiman had been considerably banged about ... The purpose of the exercise, doubtless, to prevent them from forming any idea of where they might be when finally they were set down. Well, purpose achieved, Soheil reflected. But at least they'd removed the gags and blindfolds ... He slipped into sleep ...

They came for him. Bandaged his eyes again. He felt fresh air on his face as he was led outside; then a door opened and he was piloted through it. The blindfold was removed and his two-man escort left the room.

Questioning again, clearly. But the man seated behind the desk facing him – ah, no peasant, this one. An austere face, flesh covering the bones meanly; narrow patrician nose, mouth long and thin, eyes caverned beneath a jutting brow.

Fanous gathered together his aching and famished body, yelled 'Beware now!' at his tired will: he must *find out* as much as possible; must *give* the least possible – and in one particular sphere must give *nothing at all*.

There was a chair placed ready on his side of the desk. He was ordered to sit down on it and, advancing into the room, did so. He could see the face of his interrogator more clearly now: the man's eyes were grey, their paleness startling against the dark skin –

'Soheil Fanous, eye-surgeon.' The voice deep, not particularly aggressive in tone. 'You keep strange company, in Zahlé.'

'I told your thug back there –'

'I know what you told him. It has already been checked and seems to be based on fact.'

'So why are you holding me?'

'I will tell you the reason. To do so may lead you to co-operate with us. Not that the resolution of the situation is in your hands, unfortunately for you. But by writing letters, appeals for help, to your wife, to the hospital authorities, you may perhaps be of assistance to us. Such things sometimes serve a turn indirectly …

'You, Fanous, are our pawn' – the man smiled briefly – '*one* of our pawns, held ready to be traded against our acquisition of *someone else*.'

A frequent ploy in the business of hostage-taking, of course, Fanous was aware of that; had in fact already thought about it, and had concluded it to be – in his own case – a reason preferable to other possible ones.

'Against your acquisition of "someone else"?' he enquired politely. 'Who?'

But got a question back: 'You know that the daughter of the FFP leader, Abu Hamad, was killed – assassinated – on the fourth of May, by AKAL terrorists?'

'I read about it in the papers.' Watch every word now; and guard the expression on your face.

The man behind the desk leaned forward; his eyes gleamed, a sudden malevolence in them.

'Abu Hamad wants the man who killed her,' he said. Voice quiet but loaded wih menace; and his face lit with chill pleasure as he contemplated the implicit future violence.

'Two gunmen, the report said –'

'*Not* the gunmen. They are nothing. He wants to have in his hands *the man who ordered it done*. That man is marked for death.'

It jolted Fanous. This was a scenario he had not envisaged and it bristled with sharp daggers. He held the piercing grey eyes. Kept his body relaxed. 'Where do I come into this?' he asked. 'One man, and quite meaningless to AKAL –'

'But you are one of many.' The interrogator settled back in his chair. 'Three other small cadres similar to that of Othman received orders the same as his. We now hold *eight* AKAL men, in different parts of the country.'

'I am not of AKAL. Not of any political grouping.' Lies get voiced convincingly when you are lying for your life – and should hold you safe as long as the opposition cannot actually prove them to be what they are.

'We are working on your connections. You were meeting with AKAL men when you were seized.'

'I do not deny I have had contact with AKAL, and with other Groups, militias also. I make no secret of it. As an eye-surgeon – and as a man, for that matter – I do not ask what political Group a person belongs to before I give him what help I can if he asks for it.' Truth. I wonder did it come out as convincingly as that all-important lie?

'The point will probably prove immaterial. The deal is already on the table between FFP and AKAL. Eight men in exchange for one: AKAL is expected to accept. They have to: they cannot send eight of their own innocents' – his voice sneered at the word – 'to their deaths, for the sake of one man.'

Fanous sat silent: it seemed the safest reaction. And after a moment his interrogator brought out from a drawer in the desk a pad of paper, pushed it and a pen across to him.

'You will write to your wife,' he ordered. 'I will dictate what you will say.'

Fanous made no move to pick up either. 'You will send it to her?' His tone mocked, made clear he placed no trust in any such humanitarian moves on the part of his captors.

'Perhaps.'

'But you won't move against her?'

'I know of no plans to do so. We have, naturally, established 24-hour surveillance on her apartment and on those who frequent it or live in it ... I will untie your hands, and we will proceed.'

As he began to write – clumsily, the hands having been tied for so long – Fanous' thoughts touched briefly on his wife. Were she to react too emotionally to the situation, his present deception might yet be penetrated and disaster follow? Small things she spoke of, each innocent-seeming in itself, might be taken hold of by some inimical and devious mind and woven into a damning whole...? But as he wrote on, the main thrust of his thought was one of furious anger against the men who had bungled so ruinously the attempt on Abu Hamad's life. By God, they would pay! In time, they would pay ...

'You may end with a short personal message if you wish,' the interrogator said.

But Soheil Fanous merely signed his name at the end of the dictated letter.

'So you don't actually know what's happened to him?' Lois had heard her sister's story through. Clearly, there wasn't much to tell. What there was had come out jerkily, words prised out of the mind that was absorbed in its own trauma, inward-looking, unbelieving and *refusing belief to* the implications of the known facts. And the teller now sitting back in her armchair, head resting against its rose-red velvet, her oval face curiously lax and somehow defenceless, brown eyes dull beneath the shaped arrowy brows; the long black hair, though, now meticulously arranged, swathed close to her head, gleaming. All is not lost, then, Lois thought in a flash of perception compounded of fragments of a thousand memories of Tagarid-past: so long as this beautiful sister of mine grooms her hair to perfection, she is not yet beaten however terrible the blow to her heart.

'I know only that he didn't come back from Zahlé that day. His car was found, undamaged, outside a restaurant in the town. But no-one had seen him park it there.'

'And the people at the clinic up there? Staff, patients?'

Pale long-fingered hands rose and fell in a gesture of emptiness. 'Nothing. He followed his routine and then left at his usual time.'

Lois drank the last of her coffee. Looked around her: the room had not changed in essentials since her last visit: elegantly appointed – fitting environment for Tagarid – its colours were rose-red and ivory and sage-green, its pictures good ones, its lamps shaded in silk. Tagarid's 'scene' more than Soheil's, she reflected ...

'What puzzles me is why they – whoever's holding him – haven't come out into the open.' Tagarid had got to her feet, was standing by the French windows that opened onto the balcony, her arms folded across her breast as though she sought to hold herself together, physically. 'The general assumption is that he has been abducted,' she went on. 'But to me that's nonsense, because there's no conceivable reason for any Group to do that. Soheil has no *time* for politics; no heart for it, either. That's known, it's common knowledge. For him,

his work occupies the entirety of his life and self –'
Abruptly, she broke off; and stood gazing out at the
pot-plants massed on the balcony, bright-flowered.

The room suddenly very quiet. Lois watched her
sister; saw a shiver run through her body, saw her arms
drop to her sides.

'What is it, Tarri?' The childhood diminutive she
hadn't used for ten years and more. There was no
answer; but she sensed no withdrawal either and so
after a moment went on: 'Is it that you feel there's not
much room for you now, either?' She said it because it
seemed to follow from Tagarid's last words; but voiced,
it seemed – impossible. But then, no, not impossible:
Soheil a self-proud and very complicated man, also very
virile. 'Is there another woman?' she asked.

'No! That, never! I know him –!' Tagarid rounded on
her furiously.

'What then? You brought it up, don't get angry with
me when I take up something *you* started.'

Colour back in her face, her body suddenly alive with
nervous energy, Tagarid crossed the room to stand in
front of her sister.

'No, I'm sorry. I want to talk about it. Can't, to anyone
else ...' She made a small gesture of frustration,
frowning as she went on. 'This last year, Soheil has
become too engrossed in his work. He gives too much of
himself, and of his time. Oh I admire him for it, you
know that. Love him the more because of it – you know
that, too. So does he, I've told him often enough. But I –
I want more of him for myself.' She turned away, went
over to her chair and sat down again. 'I told him that, as
well,' she said. 'But he made nice words for me and –
avoided the issue.'

'But the work he does *is* very demanding, and, well,

valuable. He's got to "give himself" to it or else he wouldn't be nearly so brilliant at it as he is.'

'Don't sound so damn pious!'

'*You're* sounding pretty damn mean! The jealous woman … To be jealous of a man's *love*' – deliberately, she emphasized the emotionally (and sexually) "loaded" word – 'for his work isn't that much different from being jealous of his love for another woman. Either way, the jealous one wants to take all, leaving nothing for anyone or anything else.'

Tagarid sat silent. Then, slowly, smiled a little. 'None of that matters at the moment, does it,' she said. 'I'm glad you're here, Lois.'

'Surely he'll be released soon, it must be a mistake of some sort. I've taken a week's leave, have to go back on –'

'A week? That's nothing!' Tagarid on her feet again, her face anguished. 'These things can drag on for ages.'

'I can't just drop everything.'

Tagarid came close to her sister and looked her in the eyes. 'Maybe he's dead already,' she said slowly. 'Or maybe they'll play cat-and-mouse, with both him and me, for months on end. You never *know*, here. For God's sake stay – a few weeks, at least. I'd go mad on my own.'

Lois stood up. 'Lebanon's toll,' she said sombrely. Then turned away and began to gather up the coffee-cups and replace them on the tray. 'I couldn't just sit around here all day,' she said, half-laughing, seeking to take the tension out of the air. 'You've got your work, you're out from 3 till 8 every day: Liliane's got her studies. Cooped up here alone, nothing to do – *I'd* be the one to go crazy …'

But by the end of that evening, Lois had discovered herself 'claimed'. Reclaimed, the truer word: she saw

Tagarid to be near breaking-point – and knew herself (as at other times of severe crisis in the past) the only person to whom her sister would be able to express her fears and dreadful uncertainties and thus find some relief, find quietness for a while, the thin short-lived peace of emotional exhaustion. As she watched Tagarid move stiffly through the hours, enclosed in her personal agony, trying to shut it away from the eyes of Liliane, of Salaam the trusted servant-of-many-years, Lois came to realize and accept that she was not going to return to Lewes, she was going to stay on in Beirut. Until Soheil – well, until an end of some sort had been reached, was known beyond doubt.

Dinner over – cooked and served and cleared away by Salaam, uncharacteristically silent throughout – Lois went out onto the balcony. Resting her arms on the balustrade, gazed out over the lit city. At night, its scars were hidden; and you could not see the uniforms – alien or native, but all battle dress – or the various 'engines of war' established in their positions of menace or defence. And the aura of the city took her for itself again, it did not even have to try very hard, it just, moved in: the place she was born in, grew up in – and in her teens had been sent away from, to a safer 'climate' ... She perceived the horror of what had happened to Soheil as an integral part of Lebanon's long ordeal: and understood then that *it was not in her* simply to walk away from it, returning to the safe and lovely life of a country at peace as if nothing of importance were being enacted in the native land of the 'other half' of her parentage.

A sudden lightness in her heart now the decision was made, she went back into the lounge. Tagarid was sitting at one end of the long settee, doing nothing at all. Liliane was at the polished oval table in the window recess, head bent over a notebook, her dark curly hair tousled.

'I'm going to stay,' Lois announced. Aware of an inner excitement.

Tagarid looked up. 'But, what *will* you do? All those hours alone.' Warily, not quite believing.

'God knows. I'll find something.' She laughed. 'Maybe I'll learn to crochet. Salaam can teach me.' It was a family "joke": Salaam did intricate and beautiful crochet-work and had once been encouraged to instruct Tagarid in the craft: both had tried hard to make a success of the lessons but results had been wretched, the long graceful fingers failing where the nimble peasant hands fashioned such exquisite things ...

And Tagarid believed, then. Smiled wih relief, and gratitude; and poured brandy for them both while they sat down and talked together. Not of Lebanon, not of Soheil. Personal talk, in shared intimacy: of Dan Ferguson, Lois' lover; of relatives of their dead parents, first of their English father's brother who had settled in Australia in the fifties and was corresponded with only fitfully, then of the numerous relations on their mother's side, all of them long since fled Lebanon and now resident in various parts of California – copious letter-writers, these, all family affairs assiduously reported to the two 'girls' left behind in the old world and consistently refusing all offers of a new life in the States, 'I have a friend here, my dear, who will guarantee you a job, excellent money and very good prospects ...'

It was Liliane who interrupted them.

'I've been thinking, about Lois staying here and being bored, with nothing to do,' she said, looking across at Tagarid. 'What about Leila? Remember the other day, she was grumbling about her staffing problems, and asked if you knew anyone who might be available to teach English at her Academy? You didn't, but –'

'Me, *teach*?' Lois began to laugh, shaking her head.

But Tagarid seized on the idea. 'Oh it won't matter that you're not trained,' she said. 'You're a native speaker, and in Leila's establishment that's pure gold … It's a language school, there's a couple of Brit girls teaching there –'

'Brit girls in West Beirut? Surely –'

'One is married to a Palestinian; five years they've been living here, I think, something like that. The other –' she considered for a moment, then dismissed the matter with an impatient gesture, going on, 'Oh I don't remember the details, but there'll be something that makes it possible for her … Lois, you'll do it? Yes?'

'Yes, then. If this Leila will have me, I don't see why not.'

Tagarid was already reaching for the phone.

Four

Leila Asly's language 'academy' was across the city, in a side-road off Bliss Street: a large mansion set amidst gardens. It was a relatively safe area since several Middle East embassies were situated nearby, each of them well guarded, both by visible armed soldiery and by clandestine agreements (the latter probably the more effective in this city where so many live and die by the gun). Leila paid protection-money to several Groups in order to carry on her establishment without interference; and charged high fees for her courses. She suffered no lack of students, especially in the English Language department: many people in the city, young and old, aimed to emigrate, to go to places such as the USA, Australia, South America, often to join relatives already citizens of those countries; others, particularly those with technical skills, sought the well-paid contract jobs open to them in the Gulf and Saudi Arabia, where English was the lingua franca of their trade.

Tagarid's telephone calls of the previous evening had prepared the way for Lois to work there, arranging teaching hours (temporarily) and rates of pay. And now at 2.30 in the afternoon she was working in a small staffroom opening off Leila's office. With her sat Geraldine Smith, and textbooks were piled on the table between them. Two of the classes Lois was to take over, beginning the next day, were following a course parallel to that of one of Geraldine's, so they had been sorting things out together (or as Lois had phrased it earlier, 'I'd like to pick your brains, please, if you don't mind'); the third was an evening class Geraldine had been wanting to 'shed' for a long time, having only accepted it in the first place to help Leila out in her ever-running battle against teacher-shortages. '2DE' this last was named – the 'D' level an advanced one – and the two of them had discussed its take-over in detail, also the students, fourteen on roll, ages ranging from eighteen to forty-five.

Geraldine clearly knew all of these well; and, in one or two cases, had learned something of the motivation behind their enrolment at the Academy. One in particular interested her, as became apparent as they talked: a young man named Fahal Rizik, Palestinian, aged twenty-four, high IQ and a student in the very best sense of the word; but desperately poor, without close relatives, and living by himself in one of the refugee areas on the south side of the city. She was still talking about him, her small, delicate-featured face vivid with her concern, blue eyes alight.

'It's a dire situation for him,' she said. 'Here's this job in Riyadh the Saudis have offered him, the pay's fantastic – comparatively – and although the initial contract's only for two years, it's open to renewal and they'd be sure to want him to stay on. And now all to be lost because after scraping together Leila's fees he can't raise the money for a visa.'

'It doesn't cost much, though, does it? Fifteen Lebanese pounds, something like that?'

A grimace of distaste. 'Five hundred more, in the back

pocket, or you don't get one.'

'Oh.' Not a great deal of money, in 'my' world, Lois thought, but probably totally unobtainable to the 'Fahal Riziks' of Beirut – except in payment for certain services, possible then, surely, but such jobs all go to 'the boys', you may be sure, I don't imagine you can just do a one-off and then hightail it out of the country.

'He's got so much going for him, personally.' (And it seemed to Lois that Geraldine had read something of her mind then; and she looked up sharply: the other girl wore her long blonde hair piled high at the back of her head and strands and wisps of it had escaped the pins, drifted against the creamy skin.) 'I really feel for him, you know. To see a chance like that slipping away from you – and such opportunities don't come often to men like him, not here, these days.'

'He can't borrow?'

'No collateral, for a business arrangement. And his friends don't have that kind of money, either ...' She got up, started gathering books together. 'I'd give it him myself if I could spare it, but I can't. I'm saving all I can to finance a post-grad course in the UK, to get a teaching qualification to go with my degree ... I feel somehow ashamed not to give it to him,' she murmured, turning away. 'But then I tell myself not to be a sentimental fool ... That's what Nizar says, too,' she added.

'Nizar?'

'He's Syrian, a major in the army here. We live together.' Books in her arms, she faced Lois again, her face flushed. 'I've got to go now,' she said hurriedly. 'Anything else you need, about the work?'

Not thinking about that, Lois shook her head. Pictures were flashing through her mind: the squalid silhouettes of the camps, seen from the airport road – Tagarid's face as she opened the door to her yesterday, broken she looked – Soheil kidnapped, the gifted hands broken also? Too many things, *broken* –

'I'll give you the five hundred pounds,' she said abruptly. 'You pass it on to him. Don't tell him it's from me. It's a gift: no repayment required, ever.'

Later, she walked back home through the city. Half an hour, it took. The first part through the well-kept, well-policed 'diplomatic' district, but that soon behind her and then the real city assaulting eyes and mind with its urban deserts of shell-craters, the sudden huge gaps looming at the sides of streets where entire buildings had been blown to pieces – and branded on walls left standing, the imprints of fireplaces and flights of stairs bearing witness to the fact that once-upon-a-time, people lived there ... She felt glad that she had given Geraldine the cash cheque on her bank. To do something positive ...

At the apartment, she found Liliane alone. Salaam had departed, leaving dinner prepared; and Tagarid had driven off at 2 o'clock to the city offices of 'Save The Children' for her daily 3 to 8 stint there, her own car vital to her particular job since it frequently required that she visit outlying areas.

'I'll make coffee while you change.' Liliane uncurled herself from the corner of the sofa and made for the kitchen; sixteen years old, she was slender, a vivacious girl possessed of boundless energy, and slightly rebellious to Tagarid's efforts gradually to inform her with adult poise.

Lois took her time, in her own room, first sorting through the notes and textbooks Geraldine had given her, then changing into casual clothes and returning to the lounge. Turkish coffee ready on the low glass-and-gilt table: the aroma fragrant on the air as she poured herself a cup.

'How's life?' she asked, looking across at Liliane who had curled herself onto the sofa once more.

'For me, good. But this is hell for Tagarid, isn't it? Pure hell.'

'I'm glad she went to work.'

'She had to assemble herself together, bit by bit, to do it … It'll be better for her when she *knows*. One way or the other – anything's better than living in limbo.'

Lois sat down, sipped her coffee. She was wondering how freely she might allow herself to talk to this girl. She did not know her well: for three years Liliane had been living with Tagarid and Soheil, adopted after both her parents were killed in some random mortar-attack. Tagarid had been assigned to help her, and had found herself drawn to the girl. And had drawn the girl to her: they had grown very close … Maybe something to do with Tagarid being childless and the girl parentless? Two negatives preparing the ground for a positive …?

'Tell me, Liliane' – she leaned forward towards the girl, her mind made up now – 'do *you* think Soheil has been abducted by one of the Groups? Tagarid argues against it so strongly, but then that's partly because she can't bear to think of him besmirched by common politics. How do *you* see it?'

The dark head bent; one hand smoothing over velvet upholstery. She knew well enough what she wanted – *ought to* say; but was not finding it easy to commit herself. At last:

'Tagarid is – is blind to certain aspects of his character, it seems to me,' she said. 'She *refuses* them.'

She looked up then – and committed herself, speaking fast, almost angrily. 'I think it quite possible that in spite of what he says he *is* a member of a Group, secretly. Which makes me think it's feasible that he's been abducted by another organization, one hostile to whichever one *he's* with.'

But Lois' curiosity had been aroused by the earlier words. 'What are these "aspects of his character" you think she's blind to?' she asked.

Liliane ran a hand through her hair, then drew up her knees and clasped her arms round them: the saying of it still wasn't easy. 'He is such an opinionated man.' She got it out, slowly. 'He's always talking about his work and it's always, somehow, the brilliance of his own performance that seems to be the object of the exercise.' She frowned, gestured a certain impatience with herself; then went on, 'He *is* brilliant, yes, I know that. But he, he parades it. He brags; and then suns himself in Tagarid's admiration ...'

'But what makes you think he might actually belong to one of the Groups?'

'Don't you see, that's part of the same thing? Could be, I mean ... He's not, it seems to me, the kind of man to devote himself entirely to his own work and leave the men of power – who are, ultimately, the Groups and those who control them – to run Lebanon ... I sense ruthlessness in him. It frightens me sometimes.'

'Have you said anything of this to Tagarid?'

'No, never.'

'She must surely know him better than you –'

'Not necessarily.' The interruption swift; and a level stare accompanying it. '*I love her.*'

'You mean – Soheil doesn't?'

But the girl would not go on. She shook her head,

swung her feet to the floor and stood up, moved across to the table where her biology books lay open.

'How did you get on at Leila's?' she asked, seating herself again.

So Lois let her escape; and related the more interesting parts of her visit to the Academy that afternoon. Finally:

'Geraldine told me she's living with a Syrian officer,' she said. 'Have you met him? Seen him?' For Liliane was studying a six-hours-a-week course at the Academy and Geraldine was her teacher.

'No. Neither. We all know about it, of course, though.' She picked up a pencil, opened a notebook in front of her. Suddenly, stilled; looked up.

'Lois!' Her voice excited. '*A Syrian officer!* Don't you see, he may be able to help, to get us some information about Soheil? He may have ways, the Syrians often know a lot more about the hostage-taking that goes on than they admit publicly ...'

When Tagarid came home later that evening, she too thought it was an avenue worth exploring.

The FFP meeting took place in a private house, in a room sombrely but expensively furnished: silk-shaded lamps, drawn tapestry curtains patterned with Persian motifs, miniatures painted on ivory grouped on a damascened wall. The door was locked – not because these leaders feared attack (that, they knew themselves well guarded against), but to forbid casual interruption. Three men, and all ambitious within the hierarchy of this pro-Iran Group: they sat in armchairs around a rosewood table. On it lay three hardbacked files, each quite thin, neatly stacked one upon the other.

' ... as yet there has been no response from AKAL to

our proposed deal.' The senior executive – a banker – sat back, his resumé of the situation completed.

'Then it is time to take action that will exert real pressure on them.' A bitter man, Mahmoud; and fierce with it, always itching for conflict – for ordering its initiation, that is, then while it was in progress taking vicarious pleasure in the resulting personal agonies and (occasional) blood: (his own family had lost a great deal of the latter in the fighting in Beirut during '82, no sons left alive to continue his name, so his lust was insatiable) … He owned a pharmacy near the Commodore Hotel.

The third man – a lawyer – sat forward, putting his question in his throaty, eager voice; he was the most junior officer present. 'Action, through which one of the hostages?' he asked, knowing that the chief would already have made his decision on that point before calling the meeting.

'Fanous. The surgeon.' It was the obvious choice to make from the eight IDs in their hands, and the other two nodded. 'He is not an active member of AKAL, but clearly he has some sort of connection there or we would not have him now. And he is a man with a considerable reputation: AKAL will not want him – or his family – to be seen to be suffering. That would lose them a degree of public sympathy; also, perhaps, it will bring calls from the man-in-the-street for our terms for Fanous' release to be agreed.'

'The man Abu Hamad is after, given into our hands, then.' Mahmoud envisaging a near future full of interesting possibilities, anticipating that the revenge enacted by Abu Hamad on the man who ordered the ambush which had caused the death of his daughter would be a satisfactorily brutal one.

'We threaten Fanous himself?' Again it was the junior

man who advanced the discussion.

'No. In this case we attack obliquely: move against those closest to him. Thus, put pressure on AKAL, for they will wish to be seen as able to protect their own. Also, to a certain extent, such action gives us a lever with Fanous himself; we can use reports of any violence employed to extract from him a communication to AKAL, begging that they agree the terms.'

Mahmoud struck to the heart of the matter. 'When do we begin?' he demanded. 'And who is to be in charge?'

'It is already in hand, in regard to surveillance of the Fanous apartment and investigation of those who live in or frequent it.' The senior man leaned forward, reached out and pushed the three files across the table towards Mahmoud. 'You take over from now on. These are the reports so far received. It appears there are three people to work on: his wife, the wife's sister – the two are half Lebanese, half Brit, dual nationality – and a girl named Liliane Ansari, an orphan they took in three years ago; she's sixteen years old, a student.'

'About the same age as Abu Hamad's daughter, then.' The junior man let his thought slip out in words. But Mahmoud spoke straight over it, his harsh voice stamping it to pieces, lost.

'Good,' he said. 'You may leave them to me.'

Five

End of class, the advanced level evening set, the students on their way out, and Lois fiddling with the recorder on her desk, the cassette seemed to be stuck in there ...

'Miss Lois.' Although she had had only two lessons with this class, she at once recognized his voice, there was a clarity and depth to it that she found most pleasing, and the Arab accent tilting her name slightly, touching it with a sort of specialness.

'Fahal.' She looked up. 'This damn thing's fouled up.' Then as she knew he would, he said, 'Let me help you'; and as she knew he would, for he was not a man easily associated with failures, he extricated the tape with little difficulty. She watched his hands, enjoying the sensitively used strength of the long brown fingers; and then her eyes moved over the compact figure, the neat profile to the face intent on its task.

Fahal Rizik placed the cassette on her desk, turned to her. 'I have been making enquiries about Soheil Fanous,' he said quietly. 'I found out nothing about his present situation. It is, covered, I think, heavily *covered*. But there is a telephone number. If you ring it, it is possible ...' He broke off, his eyes slipping away from hers for a second, towards the open door of the empty classroom; then he faced her again and went on. 'Something may develop, if you ring this number,' he said. 'I do not promise. But, I hope.'

Tense, she stared into the dark eyes: it had come so suddenly – and a shocking contrast in it, terrorist-abduction and the horrors inherent in that now ripping open the quiet self-absorption, the sheer ordinariness of classroom life; paradigms on the blackboard, Nada's perfume lingering on the air, she moved in an aura of Chanel No. 4 –

'What is the number?' she asked; and as he gave her the figures, wrote them down on the inside of the cover of her class notes, wondering, as she did so, what next …?'

'It would be a good thing to telephone soon.'

She had the feeling he was seeking to guide her (it had not yet occurred to her that he might be pushing, not simply guiding); and knew herself glad to have friendly company in this new and threatful world – yes, here in Beirut, 'world', not as in most other countries merely '*under*world' – of touch-close violence.

'Do I simply, ask about Soheil?' She put it to him evenly.

'You give *my* name. Then, identify yourself. Then, keep silent and wait. Do not say anything more until you have been responded to.' His face very still, a slight frown between the black brows. 'The number connects you only to a, a middle person. He may take time before he passes your call. You must wait with patience.'

'When shall I ring? Does it matter?'

'Have you another class now?'

She shook her head. 'I'm finished for tonight.'

'Then make the call immediately. Use the telephone at reception.'

Surprised at the lack of secrecy expected: 'That will be all right?' she asked; and then as he nodded, wondered where he stood in this affair – and why now this small door had been opened in the seemingly impenetrable wall of silence surrounding Soheil's disappearance –

'I will come with you,' he said, smiling suddenly; and picked up the tape-recorder and her books, to carry them for her. 'Stay at your side while you telephone.'

The reception desk was in the entrance hall of the Academy. A long counter of polished wood, and behind it the receptionist, Naji, checking in a pile of registers; at its far end as Lois and Fahal Rizik came in, the telephone stood unused. A group of students chattering together near the outside doors, all young, and arguing over which café-bar to go to now lessons were over. Naji would put them out when he thought it time, then lock away the hand-gun in his top right-hand drawer and go off to make coffee in his bed-sit at the rear, he was night-guard as well as receptionist ...

All this passed through Lois' head to re-establish contact with ordinary things. But then she found herself beside the phone. She picked it up and dialled the given number, not needing to refer to her notebook for it, it seemed engraved upon the inside of her skull –

'The number used changes all the time,' Fahal said, standing at her left elbow; he was still carrying her books but he had put the recorder down on the counter. 'Your call is expected, all is arranged –'

'Speak,' said a voice in her ear; and she proceeded according to the instructions Fahal had given her. When she got to the waiting part, that went on for a long time. She contained her mounting impatience – then after a moment recognized a touch of fear in it but drove it away, telling herself *This may be Soheil's life in your hands so keep in gear and moving, woman, Tagarid loves him* –

'Lois Everard, listen to the message. It comes from the FFP.' Flat voice, speaking Arabic, slow and deliberate: instinctively she turned her back on the group by the door, hunched herself over the receiver. 'On Sunday the 15th May,' the voice continued (she already knew it for a recording, the slightly 'tinned' timbre to the voice revealing that), 'you are to go to the Jameela restaurant in Shtaura. A table will have been booked in your name. Take your lunch there beween thirteen hundred hours and fifteen hundred hours. During that time you will see Soheil Fanous. He will be with other men. Our purpose in this is merely to prove to AKAL, beyond doubt, beyond question, that he is alive and in our custody. You will not approach him or make any attempt to convey any kind of message to him. Should you do so, he will be killed ... I repeat: the Jameela restaurant, Shtaura, the 15th May, between the hours of one and three o'clock. The warning – it is not necessary to repeat. I speak for the FFP. We are known as men of our word, and as men of blood when that serves our purpose.'

The line went dead. Lois replaced the receiver.

'What did they tell you to do?' Fahal asked as she turned to him. And full of excitement and gratitude – that one flick of fear forgotten, for surely she could be certain now that Soheil was alive? He must be! And in two days' time she would see him with her own eyes, then take that glad news to Tagarid! – she repeated to him the gist of the instructions she had just received.

'You know the restaurant?' he asked as she fell silent.

She nodded. 'We've eaten there before once or twice, my sister and I – and Soheil.' She shivered: Soheil

Cry Lebanon

suddenly terrifyingly *absent*; a black empty hole where there should be a living man …

She heard Fahal bidding her goodnight. Interrupted him, asking, 'Why, Fahal? Why have you – done this for us?' Forbidding herself to put to him the other question that had insinuated itself into her mind, which was, how were you *able to do* this for us?

He did not answer at once. Stood looking into her eyes and she could not read the expression on his face – then even as she watched, saw all expression deliberately expunged.

'I believe a man should repay his debts,' he said. 'He *has to* do that.'

Lois found it difficult to keep from Tagarid the affair she was now involved in, which she hoped would lead to a 'sighting' of Soheil and consequently to the lifting of the dread haunting her sister, the dread that he was already dead. Yet it seemed the wisest way to handle the situation, for to arouse expectations before there's a reasonable certainty that they will be fulfilled – surely, greater cruelty in that?

'Yet you know, Tagarid seems to be bearing up quite well now,' she said to Geraldine as they drove along the highway towards Shtaura, Beirut long out of sight and mind, the cool sunlit morning showering down beauty over the splendid slopes of the Lebanon range to their left, over the spread of country rolling away to their right, Israel somewhere across there, if you go far enough (but the mental effort successfully to accomplish that journey far greater even than the physical one would be). 'I'm surprised really how quickly she's, recovered. That first day, when I arrived, she was near to collapse … Seemed to be, anyway.' And even as she put into words that perceived ambivalence in Tagarid's present feelings, dismissed it almost angrily from her mind: telling herself that it was to be admired as showing how demanding was the struggle to present a brave face to the world, to keep your agony private and get on with the things that were there to be done.

'I think perhaps people here – in other countries, too, places where there's been years of civil strife, terror – acquire a particular sort of toughness of spirit. They've been readying themselves, probably subconsciously, for "it" – any one of the various horrors that are perpetrated in their world every day – to happen *to them*. So when it finally does, they're able to as it were slip into that prepared gear and carry on.'

' "Toughness of spirit".' Sombrely, Lois repeated the phrase. Then questioned it: 'Brutalization?'

But Geraldine was in holiday mood and brushed that aside, driving her Renault 5 fast, expertly, her blonde hair in a pony-tail fastened high at the back of her head, her clothes as 'English' as ever, a linen suit, butcher-blue and plain in style. 'Today, let's just enjoy ourselves,' she said. 'Last night was hell in my area. Bad shelling: started up just before midnight, got really heavy around three so I went down into the basement. I'm short on sleep but one's pretty used to that. Now it's Sunday. You've invited me for lunch, you're paying for the petrol: I intend to do justice to the Jameela's reputation for excellent food, to breathe clean country air and soak up some sunshine.'

'Lucky for me you could come, that Nizar's out on manoeuvres.' Wondering fleetingly: should I have told her the real reason why we are to lunch this day at 'Jameela' in Shtaura? But then pushing doubts aside and asking about Nizar Seiffuddin; about Aleppo, his home city to which three months earlier he had taken Geraldine on a family visit formal with serious intent …

The restaurant was light and airy, and not crowded. A table was reserved in her name, as those recorded instructions to her had stated it would be: it was beside the front windows and overlooked a big garden planted with trees and flowering shrubs, the main road beyond. The two women sat facing each other, Lois placing herself so that her eyes could command the whole room. Their lunch – a mazzé, local trout, kunafa – was very good. As the meal proceeded, people came and went; and all the while Lois kept vigilant watch. But Soheil did not appear.

… She repeated to the waiter that no, they did not wish to take their coffee in the orangery lounge, they preferred it to be served at their table; and when it came, spun out the drinking of it until ten minutes past three. Still, no Soheil.

'What *is* it, Lois?' Geraldine sat forward, resting her forearms on the table. 'You've been getting more and more tense this last hour and now you're positively jumpy. Tell me. You've got me up here. Now tell me why, please.'

It seemed a reasonable request, and since it had all resulted in nothing, why not? Lois told her, putting it briefly, hopelessness possessing her now, the chill of the return to a cruel reality: Soheil alive/Soheil dead? That question still there to torment Tagarid –

'Why didn't you tell me all this in the first place?' Geraldine's fair face flushed, rather angry.

'I was afraid you mightn't come, if I did … Would you have?'

'Oh yes. It's no good letting "the Events" interfere with what you want to do. If I didn't feel that way I'd have left the country long ago.'

'So let's be on our way back, then. No point in staying any longer.' Lois stood up, smoothing into place her yellow raw-silk overblouse, the matching trousers creased from sitting. She paid the bill and they left the restaurant, walking out into sunshine dusty from the passage of the day; this highway runs on down into the Beka'a Valley and into Syria, it carries a great deal of heavy transport and military traffic.

The Renault was in the restaurant's car-park sited alongside the road, separated from it by a low brick wall topped with chains.

'You're still uptight,' Geraldine observed as they walked towards it.

'*Why* should anyone *do* this?' It burst out of the frustration in her. 'It seems so futile! It makes no sense!'

But Geraldine gave a laugh, short and sharp and devoid of humour. 'Be sure it makes sense to someone, somewhere,' she said. 'They've devious minds. And some love playing cat-and-mouse.'

As they stood beside the Renault, Geraldine fumbling in her handbag for keys, a man approached them, getting out of the driver's seat of a red Honda parked directly opposite them across the interior freeway.

'Excuse me,' he said, coming to a halt beside Geraldine and addressing her quietly. A pleasant-faced young man, casually dressed, dark colours.

She regarded him coolly, closing her bag, shutting the keys back inside it (and at that movement it occurred to Lois, watching, that there might be a gun in there, also).

'I'm waiting for a friend who works in the restaurant,' the young man went on, waving a hand towards the car he had emerged from. 'I've been here about fifteen minutes –'

Lois had moved closer to him. 'So?' she interrupted harshly, an apprehension in her. 'What do you want with us?'

'Miss, I'm not about to try something.' He raised his hands in front of him, their palms towards her proclaiming "I come in peace". 'Thing is, I saw a fellow near your car as I was parking – it seemed to me he was acting suspiciously and I thought you might like to know what I'd seen.'

'Acting suspiciously? What was he doing?'

'He'd been underneath your car, maybe. He'd just come out from under, that's how it looked to me.'

Car-bomb. That's what they got me up here for – then as Lois got her panic reaction under control she saw the young man watching her curiously.

'There'd be, no reason,' she said stiffly. 'No possible reason. No.' There could be no reason, in the Soheil-thing, for anyone to attack *her* – could there? *Could there* …?

'I'll have a look under her, if you like.' He offered it politely. 'Better to be sure.'

Geraldine answered, impatient of Lois' preoccupied silence and considering it most ungracious, also. 'Please do,' she said, opening her bag for the keys. 'We'd be very grateful. I'll get out the rug, the ground's dusty –'

But he was already down on his hands and knees. Turned over onto his back and slid head and shoulders in under the chassis. Lois noted that his black shoes were scuffed; and wondered if she'd been stupid not to tell Tagarid the real reason for her trip to Shtaura …

'The car is clean.' Standing beside them once more, he brushed himself down vigorously, then straightened up. They thanked him; and he smiled upon them, a young man pleased to have been of assistance to two (attractive) ladies in distress. 'I'll go in the restaurant now, see what's keeping my friend so late,' he said, and left them, sauntering away towards the rear entrance. Turned once, saw them still watching him, and waved; walked on, then, and out of their lives.

They got into the Renault. Then just as Geraldine was about to switch on –

'Wait!' Lois cried, grabbing sideways at her hand, pulling it away from the ignition. 'God! Don't you see, all this could have been a ploy? Maybe that man wasn't what he said he was! Maybe what he did was designed *to stop us from looking under there!*'

Geraldine stared at her: saw her face drained of colour, her eyes narrowed, a feral look in them as though she knew herself living in a world where predators stalked her every move, waiting their chance. 'You're letting things get to you,' she said steadily. 'Letting *Beirut* get to you. Make you scared all the time.'

Lois' mouth thinned. 'Beirut.' She repeated the name of the city, softly (and Geraldine saw her hands were shaking). Nodded then, shifted in her seat. 'Yes, Beirut. Which is why I'm going to get out of this car and see for myself.'

'D'you know what to look for?' Geraldine trying to ridicule her out of it.

'I know what to look for. Soheil taught us all, back in '87, one time there was a scare.' She was opening the door.

'Then take the rug or you'll get filthy.'

'If there's anything, we'll call the police.'

But there was – of course? – no device of any kind fixed in position under the Renault.

... Lois re-folded the rug and tossed it in the back, then got into the car once more.

Watching her from the secrecy of the rear seat of the red Honda, the FFP man smiled to himself. Small stuff, all this of softening up Fanous' women, he reflected. But he'd work his way up into the big-time ... Today, objective achieved: Lois Everard was a frightened woman. Oh doubtless she would master her fear, probably already had. But she would be unlikely to forget that, however briefly, *fear had mastered her*, which would make her – and those others in the apartment, Fanous' close ones, to whom she would surely confide these events – that much more tractable when the time came to use them ...

That evening the man in charge of the secure captivity of Soheil Fanous, and of his interrogations when that was thought necessary or desirable, sat down behind his large teak desk and considered the present state of the affair, prior to calling Fanous in for further questioning – routine merely, it would be, for it seemed clear by now that Fanous had indeed had only superficial contact with AKAL, was therefore in no position to be aware of the identity of the man Abu Hamad was attempting to flush out into the open, the man who had ordered that ambush of 4th May, when AKAL had gunned for Abu Hamad himself but instead had killed his daughter ... Nevertheless, Fanous was a useful hostage to hold; and pressure might yet be brought to bear on AKAL *via his relatives*. So keep at him; weaken him; and, hopefully, finally *use him* ...

He sent for the captive. Ordered his blindfold removed but the hands left as they were, tied behind the back; and that he be allowed to sit down in the chair placed ready for him across the desk.

Then, related to him the simulated attack which had

been mounted that day against his sister-in-law Lois Everard.

Fanous listened with obvious concern (and by the end was ready with his considered reaction).

'But she is visiting us only! It is unjust to involve her in this matter!' Righteous indignation, and a carefully calculated amount of dutiful anxiety.

'AKAL was unjust to "involve" ' – he inflected the word with implications of its cruel past and of its future ugly possibilities when applied to those associated with AKAL – 'the daughter of Abu Hamad, if you take my meaning … Now you will answer some questions …'

It seemed there was nothing new to ask; and the answers Fanous gave (since he was a man possessed of both a quick mind and an excellent memory) contained merely the information he had given when replying to them on the previous occasions. Nevertheless, he was conscious that he was beginning to find it more difficult to retain his mental agility during these sessions, more of a strain properly to monitor his responses without the trained mind that was attacking him suspecting the extent to which he was doing so …

At last the end came. The guard was summoned, the blindfold re-tied. Fanous was jerked to his feet and led to the door. As he reached it, (hearing the guard's hand on the knob) words slashed at him from behind.

'The next time, the strike against your family will be for real, Fanous.' The interrogator's voice edged with the anger in him. 'AKAL would do well to accept our terms soon. If not, their friends will suffer. And be publicly seen to suffer. That is bad for a Group. It leads – understandably – to a considerable falling away of support.'

Fanous had stopped in his tracks. Head down, was

fighting to a standstill the fury surging inside him; words of ferocious challenge sprang to his tongue – but he bit down on them ... After a moment, was able to relax. Thanked God for the blindfold hiding his eyes, for the ropes binding his wrists. Licked his lips; and said, nothing. Straightening then, heard the guard open the door; was pushed through it and felt a cool breeze on his face.

Returned to his cell – alone in it now, he and Suleiman had been separated three days earlier – he stretched himself out on the wooden bed, lying on his side, working his shoulders until he had achieved a modicum of comfort.

And congratulated himself on the way he was holding his own against the FFP interrogator. More than just 'holding his own': he was winning! Successfully deceiving him, had already convinced him that he, Soheil Fanous, did not possess the information they sought, namely the identity of the man who had ordered the ambush of Abu Hamad's car; also that he was but a fringe member of AKAL – and therefore of no individual use to them in the pressuring of that Group. No mean achievement ...

So, he thought, the FFP are hitting out now. Lois Everard; probably Tagarid and Liliane next ... Well none of them know *anything*. Thank God for that. Years ago I got it firmly established with AKAL that *under no circumstances* are they ever to tell Tagarid about me. And since because of that she has no information to give, nothing the FFP may do to her, or to Lois or Liliane, can possibly result in any harm coming to me, or to 'my people'. I'm safe as far as that goes. Let the FFP do their worst in that direction. It will perhaps serve to keep their minds off more important things ...

Six

'You telephoned the police as usual this morning?' Lois thrust the question – it was an idle one, since she knew Tagarid would at once have reported to her any change in the situation – into the silence that had gathered itself into a tight knot between herself and her sister. They were lying on sunbeds on the balcony, Tagarid in a bikini, Lois in "school" clothes, but the tan linen skirt pulled high above the knee, the blouse unbuttoned. In half an hour she would have to be on her way to the Academy, afternoon class at 3 o'clock.

'Of course. Nothing new ... "Hostages to fortune" ' – she murmured the words dreamily (and Lois, looking at her curiously, saw her eyes closed against the sunlight, her long dark hair pushed free of her neck and fanning out across the flower-patterned cushion cover) – 'That's what he said, Soheil.'

'In reference to what?'

'Children ... Always he'd say the time wasn't right. That there was war in the land and he didn't see much hope of peace for a long time. But that day, I kept at it. I'd been thinking about it a lot, that I was thirty years old and ... Well, I kept at it.' (Lois sitting very quiet. Her sister had always fought shy of emotion, of expressing her own feelings, particularly sexual ones: past experience warned that if interrupted now she would clam up, shut herself away.) 'I said that he and I had no part in politics so why should that influence us? I said that I loved him for his devotion to his work, and for his deliberate distancing of himself from politics, his refusal to commit himself to any one political grouping lest such a stance diminish his usefulness as a surgeon, restrict it ...'

She fell silent for a moment. Then opened her eyes, propped herself up on one elbow and faced her sister.

'But he turned away from me so I left it,' she said, her voice suddenly harsh, her face wiped clean of all expression. 'I could see I was beginning to annoy him and that was horrible so I left it.'

Lois frowned, meeting the brown eyes. 'When was this, then?'

'Early March. Daffodils and strawberries on the street stalls ... Two months later he was abducted.' Abruptly, she looked away, lay back again. Closed her eyes.

This time, Lois let the silence continue. She was puzzled, and oddly apprehensive. Tagarid's attitude to Soheil's disappearance, her behaviour sometimes during these last few days, seemed more than a little curious: she seemed *angry* about the abduction (which had not yet in fact been established as an abduction), but in a peculiar way, it was an anger with a touch of discontent tainting it, making it somehow a lesser thing ...?

Soon, then: 'I must be going or I'll be late.' She spoke quietly, getting to her feet. And Tagarid said she would be back home by eight-thirty that evening, said for Lois to take care, after what had happened up at Shtaura the day before, to take great care; but she did not open her eyes.

On her way to the Academy, walking the sunny wounded streets of the city, Lois' thoughts moved on from her sister, to herself, the two of them linked by blood yet so different from each other ... Tagarid shutting her emotions up inside herself, afraid that 'telling' might render her vulnerable, that the person who 'knows' will almost certainly, in time, use that given knowledge as a weapon against her ... While I, Lois, I give (*she* says) too much, too easily. True, maybe. Not that I've given without reservation – not yet (except to Tagarid!). Body and lots of close-talk, yes, that, to Dan Ferguson (strange how little I've thought about him since I got here – proves my point, I suppose). But not yet have I experienced that other giving: that indefinable 'other' which – I imagine – takes and holds and is for ever, gut, heart, self, all given and taken and you know it is for life.

Fahal Rizik was in class as usual. Lois walked into the classroom at six o'clock and he was in his place, front row, the desk beside the window overlooking the garden. At sight of him she felt a slight physical shock, a momentary disorientation; yet she had expected he would be there. Why should he not be? He was a paid-up student and, as she was well aware, was hungry for the lessons. Carefully, she smiled at him and then trailed the smile over the rest of the class; then plunged into the sometimes infuriating sometimes exhilarating give-and-take of teaching. And in giving the whole of herself to that, entirely forgot Shtaura and car-bombs and the fear which lingers on inside you long after you have made quite sure there isn't one there – fear lying in wait round corners, jumping you with 'if it *had* been' horrors ...

Several students stayed behind after class, pausing at her desk to chat, to ask questions relating to the work just done; but finally there was only Fahal.

'I am sorry that the Shtaura trip was bad,' he said, brown eyes steady on hers. 'What happened was not of my doing.'

'I don't want to talk about it.' Added spitefully, 'Not to you, anyway.'

'Please believe me, I did not know what was to happen.'

'Well you know now. Let's leave it, shall we.'

Swiftly, he changed to Arabic. 'I do not want to leave it "there", because in that place you and I are enemies,' he said. 'We are not enemies, Miss Lois, it is not in us to be enemies.' He reached out and gathered up her books from the desk, to carry them for her. 'Please let us talk together,' he went on, quietly, hurriedly. 'There is a café along the street. Take a cup of coffee with me.'

'What would we talk about?' But the resentment had gone out of her eyes (and he saw that).

He had the books tucked under his arm, was waiting for her (in two senses, as they both perceived now). 'I would like you to understand how I came into this affair; and why. To understand something of – me.' So, Fahal Rizik laid it on the line; standing in front of her in his young easy grace, the compact body lithe, the face clear-cut in feature, an eager look to it.

'All right,' she said. Rationalizing this reversal of her original intention to attack, to accuse him, by telling herself that it was surely only fair to give him a chance to put the matter to her from his point of view.

The café was called 'Sesame': a small self-service place, it was quiet at that hour of the evening. They ordered coffee at the counter; and when it was served,

carried their cups across to a table set against the far
wall and sat down there, opposite each other.

'Tell me the how and the why, then,' she challenged
him; and studied him, having positioned herself with
her back to the wall-lights so that his face would be the
one exposed, hers the one shadowed to secrecy.

He did not answer her at once. Sat with his head bent,
staring down at the cup of coffee in front of him. His
hands were on the table beside it, big hands they were,
the fingers long and lean, strong-looking. As if they live
a lot of doing, Lois thought; wondered then what his
work was – and realized that she'd never asked
Geraldine about that job in Saudi, the one Fahal had
been offered, the one her own money was going to help
him take.

She looked up from his hands and found him
watching her, sharp-eyed.

'The "how",' he said crisply, 'is that I was approached
by a man and asked to give you that telephone number
and instruct you to call it within certain specified times –
and to see that you did so. The "why" is that in the event
of my refusing to do as asked, my visa for Saudi would
never be granted to me. But *never*.'

'But you had the money for it, *and* the "sweetener" –'

'You can't be that simple-minded!' Angrily, he threw
it at her, his mouth twisting in contempt, his eyes cutting
into hers. 'In Beirut other pressures abound; if someone
high enough up orders "No visa to this man", then *no
visa is issued!*'

Their eyes locked. Violence in him: it came at her,
malevolent, she sensed in him a trapped secret self that
craved to lash out, to hurt and maim and destroy –
anything that got in his way. *Anything*. And in that
moment understood with her blood and her bones the

true horror of the fifteen-year-long trauma of Beirut, which is, *the suborning of the people to the acceptance of violence and terror as their way of life* ... He is twenty-four, she thought, sitting shocked to the soul, and he has been breathing-in that violence and terror, touching them, smelling them, since he was a child.

Exerting her will, she turned her head away. 'Are you a member of one of the Groups?' she asked.

'Yes,' he said at once. 'That's the main reason why I want to get out of here, go somewhere else. That way I can leave the Group and no questions asked ... No punishment administered.' The amendment bitter, self-mocking (and she perceived his fear of punishment – also that he hated and despised himself for that fear). 'Don't ask me which Group,' he went on, 'it's not basically important and I don't know anything about Soheil Fanous.'

'I wasn't going to ask you about him. We came for coffee and to talk about – you and me ... Didn't we?'

It quietened him. He looked down; and after a moment picked up his cup and drank from it. But only a mouthful, then:

'That tastes horrible,' he said. 'Cold.' Looked across at her and smiled, getting to his feet and reaching out for her cup and saucer. 'I'll get us another,' he said. 'We'll drink it and tell each other the story of our lives.'

Later, he walked with her to Shams House. They walked side by side but carefully not touching. The streets were quiet. They also, quiet. Both aware that a tenuous commitment had been made, each to the other; and both a little afraid of this new thing, eyeing it warily for present and future possibilities of betrayal.

Standing on the pavement outside the apartment block, he watched her walk away from him across the courtyard, go in through the glass-and-chrome doors.

Then he turned and hurried home, to his room in the boarding-house. He had never before in his life felt so lonely. He had told her lies and he had told her truths; but it seemed to him that the lies although almost certainly the fewer in number had nevertheless somehow swallowed up the truths and established their dominion over him, he was become their creature.

As in Pharoah's dream: the lean kine eating up the fat kine and then famine rules the land ...

Lois went to bed early that night. Slept at once and did not dream –

Is pitched out of sleep by gut-fear. Jerks upright in her bed, noise smashing at and into her, a rumbling shudder, the shattering of glass and outside the curtained window a brilliance that shouldn't be there, that flares and billows redly; *there is fire in the street!*

Scrambling out of bed she rushes to the window, snatches muslin and jerks it aside; looks down on shadowy havoc lit with flame for in the centre of the line of parked cars, directly opposite the apartment, one car is ablaze, an incandescent ball of fire from which burning debris spews out – then even as she stares, appalled, that car *explodes*.

As she tugs on trousers, sweater: This time the car-bomb was for real, she thinks. And thrusts bare feet into shoes and rushes out of her room: get down there fast, people could have been hurt, nearly three o'clock, yes, but fire and flying glass – ah God, *get down there!*

But as she ran into the lounge, the phone rang. She picked up the receiver.

'Tagarid Fanous?' Man's voice, quiet, expressionless; and going on before she could answer. 'You are safe this time. Next time – well, who knows.'

And then the click of the replaced receiver.

*

The conference took place in the basement of a large block of flats on Rue 22. The greater part of this was taken up by the practice-range and weapon store, but strategically placed towards its rear was a room set aside for other purposes; sometimes interrogations were carried out there (a small 'punishment cell' opened off it, was suitably equipped) and occasionally, as on this day, it was used by executives of AKAL for discussion of current war-games.

Four men present: the two commanders sitting in leather-cushioned chairs at the table in the centre of the room, the two henchmen attending them at ease on either side of the door.

'First point. It has been decided that it is time for us to contact Fanous' wife.' The older man's delivery authoritative, he spends most of his time giving orders to underlings, and is unmarried. Sits relaxed, a powerfully-built man but his body going to seed now, belted firmly into the khaki-drill jacket. He lives near the apex of the AKAL hierarchical pyramid and the man he is addressing fears him considerably for he is known to be highly devious in his dealings with – and use of – lesser men: his loyalty to AKAL is absolute, but that apart, he pursues a merciless self-interest.

The man facing him across the table advanced the conversation circumspectly, observing quietly, 'Fanous has always stipulated that his wife must be kept in ignorance of his political involvement.'

Badr's mouth tightened. 'Fanous will have to lump it,' he replied. 'It is possible that the FFP have communicated with the woman. If they have, we'll want all the details from her.'

'But if she is not in his confidence … Well, she may not, as it were, be willing to co-operate with us.'

'Then we shall find ways to persuade her to willingness.'

The younger man persisted; he had no wish to be part of any actions which might, later, turn out to have been mistaken. 'But she is his *wife!* If we disobey his long-established directive concerning her cognizance of his true colours, reveal to her the real Fanous – and if we then force her in any way; later, Fanous may gun for us. He is not a man to take kindly to having his express instructions disregarded.'

Badr stared at him bleakly. 'Fanous is arrogant; and given to boasting.' He voiced his opinion balefully (causing the younger man to rebuke himself mentally for his momentary forgetfulness of the long-standing jealousy, the rivalry between the two men for recognition as acknowledged second-in-command that had made under-the-skin enemies of Badr and Fanous). 'She is his wife. As such it is her bounden duty to support him in *whatever he decides to do and be*. That, and to bear his children …'

The younger man sat silent. He was wondering about Fanous' wife. If she were 'wifely' in the sense Badr had just put forward, all would be well. But suppose she were not? Suppose she defied AKAL, refused her co-operation? He knew from experience that Badr held that 'he who is not with us *is against us*' – and then counted every such enemy slain as one small victory to himself … Now, hearing Badr's pronouncements on wifely obligations, he extended their implications in his mind, asking: but by the same token, Fanous is her husband – so what about *his* duties to *her*? And this man realized wih surprise that for himself that was an entirely new thought, it broke into unknown territory and who could foresee what future lay in it? He, like

Badr, had until now assumed an exclusively one-way stream-of-loyalty in such matters between husband and wife. Strange that now –

'You will go to Tagarid Fanous tomorrow.' – (Badr's voice, so it has to be listened to.) – 'Go alone, and see that you speak to her alone ... Now, to the main point of this meeting,' he went on briskly. 'FFP are pressing us hard. They have Fanous, yes, but thanks to God they do not know the truth of him. Our next move has been decided upon. It is to be implemented at once. We shall play them at their own game. Thus ...'

Succinctly, he outlined the details of the next move to be taken by AKAL.

When he fell silent, the younger man sat unmoving, his face a rigidly controlled mask. 'Such action could well start a bloodbath,' he stated flatly. 'FFP may come at us in jihad.'

'There won't be time for that, provided we act fast as soon as our new position is assured. FFP will be forced to trade.'

'And if they still refuse?'

Badr shrugged, smiling thinly. 'Should they decide *not* to trade, they won't bother with a formal refusal, I think. They'll start shooting, tell us that way.'

War in the streets *again*: for a second the younger man felt himself engulfed in a surge of despair, and he looked away –

'We'll be ready for them.' Exultation in Badr's voice.

The younger man put his shoulders back. 'Sure,' he said, echoing the laugh. 'They'll never get the better of us. We have right on our side.'

Seven

When Lois set out for the Academy at half-past nine the next morning, cleaning-up was well advanced in the area affected by the car-bomb. The amount of explosive used had been relatively small, and the chosen time of 3 a.m. had meant that there had been no people on the street or in parked vehicles: casualties had been minor ones, caused in the neighbouring dwellings by blast and flying glass. But the wreckage and desolation, the foul all-pervading smell of violent destruction – these had been with her through the later hours of the night, through the early hours of daylight as she helped neighbours quiet their children, sweep up broken glass, bandage cuts and brew hot drinks for anyone who came in, and for the personnel of the various emergency services as and when needed.

As she made her way through the chaos of burnt-out cars, of water-pumps with their fat hoses snaking across the slippery pavements, she found the filth and the smell still foully present. But the people –? Looking around her, she was amazed at the busy – cheerfulness? Can it really be that, she asked herself; and was answered: Yes, there is in them a fierce and desperate cheerfulness. They are *making it happen* in themselves; they are determined not to allow all this to dominate them ... No deaths, thank God; deaths would make it a great deal harder ...

The Academy seemed to her that day to fizz with vitality. When she reached the door of her classroom – it was to be a two-hour lesson, the medium level course – she was met by a small deputation, three of her students: Alia, a woman in her thirties, very smart and not lacking cash, who wrote stories for a magazine; Hassan, a barrister, by far the oldest in the class at forty-five, neat, dapper, very serious about his studies; and Nehmet, twenty years old and studying agriculture, her proudest boast as yet that she could drive a tractor.

'Miss Lois, we ask a favour from you,' Hassan began in slow, accented English. But then he gave an exclamation of impatience and went on in Arabic. 'We, your class, want to give a party for Nada,' he said. 'Today is her birthday and – well, there will be no party for her at home. So we have all brought cakes, and had the porter arrange for coffee and cold drinks. The others appointed we three as emissaries, and we beg that the second half of the lesson may be Nada's birthday-party. Just a little one to let her know we feel she is our sister.'

Nada: Lois recalled her. A vivacious, pretty girl of eighteen, good at spoken English, slapdash in written work; she dressed in bright clothes and was a joyous personality – until now. She had been absent last Friday. Then had appeared again yesterday, Monday: pale-faced, red-eyed, her exuberant hair scraped back into a pony-tail and her clothes of unrelieved black. After class, Lois had asked Hassan the question; and learned that Nada's eldest brother had been shot dead during the night of the previous Thursday, a petty street-battle between fringe gangs supporting rival Groups.

So Lois gave her permission for the party; and quickly improvized a mini-lesson on the giving and acknowledging of invitations – found it spilling over into animated discussions on various celebrations and their attendant special foods, then into favourite national dishes, for in the class were Lebanese, Palestinians, Syrians, one Pakistani and an Egyptian …

'We have learned many new English,' Nehmet said to Lois as they drank mango-juice together during the break between the two hour-long sessions. 'But it is my opinion, Lois, that you have learned a lot of nice cooking …' Then, "the party" was held; and in a little while Nada smiled palely and schooled herself to forget for a time, reaching out cautiously to touch and explore the strange shape of this brief period of freedom from grief …

In the staffroom, afterwards, Lois put her books away in her locker, stood at one of the open windows giving onto the garden of the old house: jasmine scent drifting in, and frangipani coming into bud, roses –

'*Good news*, Lois!' Geraldine slammed an armful of books down on a table, and reached back an arm to push the door closed behind her. Came over to the window as Lois swung round to face her (seeing her flushed, her face alight, and her hair escaping from its pins, as usual by the end of class). 'Soheil Fanous is alive!'

'You know it *for certain*?' That is the point: you hope, but it would be marvellous to know for sure. The difference between the two is enormous, like that between sleeping and the tortured hours of sleeplessness.

'Certain sure, yes!'

'Thank God.' She shook her head. 'How did you find out?'

'Nizar. I asked him – as you asked me to – and he put some feelers out through Syrian Intelligence. Anyway, I've just had a phone call from him, he says Soheil's being held by the FFP, he's definitely alive, and okay. But we're all to keep quiet about it for the moment.'

Lois leaned back against the window-sill (sun on her back and the scent of jasmine lovely). She smiled and said it was wonderful news and to thank Nizar; but the question had to be asked.

'The FFP are hard-line pro-Iran,' she said slowly. 'Why should a Group like that kidnap Soheil? They only abduct when there's political gain to be had from it, and Soheil is strictly and publicly a-political. Has been ever since I knew him.'

Geraldine turned away. 'How can you be sure of that?'

'Well, me, maybe, no. But Tagarid –'

'How can *she* be sure?'

It jolted Lois. She countered the shock of it with quick anger:

'They're close to each other! He'd have had to be living a lie every moment he was with her! And that for six years!'

Geraldine slipped her jacket off its hanger and slung it round her shoulders. Then turned again, her blue eyes cool, not offering very much.

'It happens,' she said flatly. 'In the state Lebanon is in today, most people find they can't actually stay on the sidelines for ever. But it is possible to appear to do so, if that suits your purpose … And providing you possess the necessary duplicity.' She paused at the door, smiled then. 'Anyway, he's alive,' she said gently. Made as if to say more but – did not. Went out, closing the door behind her.

Lois stood looking out over the garden again. Soheil involved in some way with the warring Groups of the city? It seemed impossible. And yet what Geraldine had just implied was true, she knew that: the 'heavy' Groups seldom took a hostage unless they thought that through their use of him they would be able to attract to themselves either some political clout or some inter-factional advantage; and a 'pure' civilian hostage would be unlikely to give them either of those. Then there was Geraldine's veiled suggestion that Tagarid must know –

Tagarid! The name triggered action: Lois sped downstairs into the street and took a taxi back to the apartment, eager to see her sister's face. She let herself in with her key, went straight through the hall and into the lounge. Tagarid was sitting at the table, hands clasped in front of her, head down; Liliane was curled in a corner of the sofa, hugging her knees.

'Soheil's alive!' Lois said breathlessly. 'He's –'

'I know.' Tagarid looked up and her face was tight, closed against the world. 'He's alive and a hostage in the hands of the FFP.'

'One man only, but he was entirely convincing. An air of authority – and of *knowing*.' Tagarid hadn't moved, but now sat back in her chair, face averted. She wanted – needed, that was apparent to Lois – to talk about what had happened here in her home that morning. 'He came about ten, you two had both left; and was gone long before Salaam arrived as usual at eleven.'

'Did he just – tell you, and go?' Inane question; but better than the thickening silence.

But the silence assembled itself again. In her place, Liliane shifted position slightly, ran her hands through her curly hair. She knew what was coming next; and looked from one to the other of the two women, desperately wanting to bring solace to them but not knowing how to do that.

At last: 'He told me that Soheil is a member of AKAL.' Tagarid looked round. 'A highly-placed and active member of AKAL.' She sent the words into the empty quietness surrounding her: to her they seemed grotesque, possessed of grim and totally unacceptable horror.

For a second Lois stared. Then: 'That's not true!' It burst out of her; but she was not sure she believed it.

'There's something about Soheil I've never told you. He *was* at one time – was AKAL. Back in '75, he was twenty then. He told me about it, before we were married. He was witness to things, did things himself, too, he said ... Then there was one particular, killing; and he ... Well, I don't know' – (but she did, you could see she did) – 'only that he got out after that. Got out of AKAL and refused to go back and ever since has loathed the Groups and all their works ... Don't you see' – face and voice anguished, she demanded her sister's understanding – 'it's *because* he had been a part of it, *because* he'd taken part in such brutalities himself, that he came to hate the whole "Establishment" here – which is the Groups – so much?'

'It makes sense.' Lois crossed the room, put a hand on her sister's shoulder. 'But never mind that now, it's not important. You haven't told me *why* this man came here – oh, to bring you the news, yes, but marvellous as it is to know he's alive it doesn't really advance things much, does it? Someone could have phoned to tell you that.'

Tagarid got up; moved slowly to an armchair, and lowered herself into it. 'You're right, of course,' she said. 'He came with a more self-interested purpose. He

wanted me to tell him all I knew about Soheil's recent
activities – recent Group contacts, that is.'

'But you couldn't –'

'No. So he, interrogated me.' She shrugged. 'I got
very hostile at that. I told him it was nonsense to say
Soheil is an activist, a highly-placed executive in the
AKAL hierarchy ... He was very angry by the time he
left. Trying not to show it, but I could tell. He left me a
phone number, said I was to ring it when I decided to
confide in them. I put it down in the book –'

'But why should he ask *you* about Soheil? Surely if he
is in AKAL, they'd know all that?'

'He told me AKAL is in touch with the FFP about the
situation. I pressed him to tell me more, but got
nowhere.'

At that moment, Salaam came in carrying a tray
loaded with cups and saucers, sugar, sliced lemon, a pot
of tea. A middle-aged woman of Syrian birth, she had
worked for Tagarid for five years, from 11 a.m. to 5
p.m. daily, doing the shopping, laundry and cleaning,
preparing the food for the evening meal, ready for
Tagarid to cook when she returned home around eight
o'clock. She was small and dark, plump, with a round
merry face and bright brown eyes; a pleasant and
dependable person, fully trusted by the family. Now,
she put the tray down on the table and busied herself
with pouring out cups of tea and handing them round.

'There was a news-flash five minutes ago,' she said
(they could hear her radio going in the kitchen now the
door was open, music: Salaam left it on all the time she
was in the apartment). 'An FFP man has been
kidnapped, they think by AKAL. Happened in
Raouché, early this morning –'

'An important man? Did it say?' Tagarid suddenly

sitting very straight; almost composed once more, but nervous tension sharpening her voice.

'No names, but they said he was one of the high-ups. A proper shoot-out, four passers-by dead ... I'll go and refill the pot, madame, you might all like another cup ...'

'Hostage-taking, a shoot-out and four innocent people gunned down – oh yes, do make sure there's plenty of tea, if you please, we may need it.'

But Lois could discover no bitterness in her sister's tone as she spoke the words; and watching her face saw it return to its customary serenity, the command of self completely re-established (the guard up again, she reflected, yes Tagarid always was like that ... So that sometimes you wonder ... Even me, I wonder ...?).

'This man from AKAL,' she said. 'Did he give you any idea what's behind Soheil's abduction? What the terms are for his release?'

'I asked, of course. He wouldn't say.'

'*Wouldn't?*'

'So it seemed to me. Not couldn't – *would* not. Which encouraged me, in a way.'

'Sure, because if what you're thinking's right and they *are* talking terms, then basically both sides must actually want an agreement. And that gives grounds for hope –'

'Lois!' Tagarid's interruption incisive. 'I've had a letter from Soheil. It came day before yesterday.'

'Why didn't you tell me? What did he say, for God's sake?'

Tagarid looked away. 'Nothing really. That's why I didn't tell you.'

'He must have said something!'

'That he was alive and being well treated by his captors. That I was to answer any questions anyone asked me about him –'

'You *knew* he was alive and kept quiet!' Mounting anger, and out of it accusation.

'Don't be naive. It could have been written the day they took him. Maybe they killed him immediately after he'd written it.'

'Well you know now, they didn't.'

'Yes, I know that much … I must ring Geraldine, and thank her. I'll do it now.' And Tagarid got to her feet and crossed the room, lifted the receiver and dialled. Was answered, and began making suitable expressions of gratitude …

Listening, watching her sister, Lois thought: I don't really know her, do I? She is still a very secret person, keeps herself so. 'Gives' to only one human being: Soheil. And that giving is the whole of herself, *offered*.

She went off to her own room. Began to write a letter to Dan Ferguson, her lover, by this time returned to England. But discovered that she had nothing to say to him: and after a while, tore up the half-page written on the theme 'I miss you' because as she read it over she realized that none of it was true.

After the 6 to 8 evening class, Lois and Fahal Rizik went again, together, to the café 'Sesame'. Sat at the same table as on the previous evening, and drank lager. Talked first about the job awaiting him in Saudi: he'd be a computer programmer with an engineering firm, he told her, and all was going well with the processing of his papers; provided it continued that way he expected to be able to take up the appointment in a month's time.

'*Provided* it does?' She looked across at him, frowning, a sudden suspicion in her that he had been, perhaps, less than truthful with her the day before. Certain questions began to form in her mind. 'Surely, *now*,

there's no doubt about it going through? That one thing
– Shtaura – that was the whole "price" of your visa? The
price you paid the FFP not to block it?'

'It was the whole price … I see you do not trust me,
Lois.'

'Should I? Would I be wise to?'

He reached out and brushed his hand lightly across
her forearm where it rested on the table – a brief touch
only (yet her skin felt newly alive where his fingers had
touched it).

'I don't think wisdom comes into it,' he said. 'Trust
comes from the heart, not the head.'

Trite; a con job; lush sentimental phraseology: all
these dismissive descriptions of his observation pre-
sented themselves to her mind but they did not win her
acceptance. Nevertheless, she asked him one of her
questions.

'Tell me one thing, please,' she said, regarding him
straitly. 'Are you committed to any further – actions – in
the matter of Soheil Fanous?'

'I am not.' His narrow-boned face open to her. 'And
having said that, I've a question of my own, to ask you,'
he went on. 'Do you believe my denial?' He demanded it
softly, holding her eyes.

Half-formed thoughts and uncertainties flashed
through her head. Deliberately, she put them aside.

'I believe,' she said. Because I want to: that *not* said;
but fingering the mind, haunting the self.

For a moment they stayed locked together within a
shared silence. Then Fahal smiled.

'What's Fanous like?' he asked. 'I've never met him,
never even heard his name until all this began.'

Lois sat back; and told him about the Soheil Fanous
known to her – known to her, that is, up till eight hours

ago! The good-looks. The well-knit figure: the physical fitness he gave time to preserving, playing squash twice a week, not as a sport but as the least time-consuming way available to him to keep his body and senses in peak condition ... The eyes that looked at people deeply and somehow, when he chose to exert their power, drew others to him ... The special gift informing his hands-brain-self, and his total devotion to the use of that gift ... His steadfast refusal to have anything at all to do with politics: some words of his which she remembered, 'I possess a talent which can benefit a great many people and I have the intelligence and trained ability which enables me to use that talent to the full; I will allow *nothing* to steal my time and my self from the proper exercise of my skill.' ... That same steadfastness there too in his refusal to leave Lebanon, he turning down all offers made to him from the U.S. and other countries, their glowing inducements – in both opportunities for research and practical experience – all rejected ... His castigation of those who fled Lebanon, taking their cash and their expertise with them to benefit 'safer' lands –

Lies, a lot of it, apparently. Lies –

'And his wife?'

The interruption – and that particular question – unexpected and disorientating. She sipped her lager, re-directing her thoughts; and after a moment began describing Tagarid to him.

'Not her looks.' He interrupted her again. 'I have seen her once, she came to the Academy to speak with Madame Leila.' He smiled. 'So you see I know she is very beautiful,' he said.

'She loves Soheil. She's passionately in love and also – I don't know quite how to put it, she *honours* him for that absolute giving of himself to his work which I was talking about just now ... In all things, she *identifies with* him.'

But he drew away from that, asking, 'Are you close, as sisters?'

She considered it, wanting to give him a full and proper answer (yes I do enjoy talking with him, it seems to make everything we discuss more real, more immediate to me – and there is a sadness in that which I don't want to define, yet). Finally:

'Yes,' she said, linking her hands on the table, looking down at them. 'We were very close, as children, and up until our late teens. Then, she went to college in France. Me, I went to college in England ... Tagarid is like our mother, leaning more to the French and Arab influences. I'm like our father and I'm drawn to the Anglo side ... But yes, we hold fast to one another.' Her eyes came up to Fahal's and she smiled suddenly. 'She has only to call and I come running,' she said. 'Always will.'

He saw the warmth in her face, the mouth smiling – to him, yes, but not 'for' him, 'for' the woman Tagarid, wife to Soheil Fanous. And tucking the knowledge away in his brain, turned his mind to other things – to Lois and Fahal *now* (let whatever may lie in the future keep to its station there, *now is for us*).

'Will you come with me to Baalbek on Sunday?' he asked abruptly, harshly almost. 'Drive up, I can borrow a car ... Please come,' he urged, seeing her hesitate but seeing her face light up, nevertheless. 'It's wonderful, the site, now there aren't any tourists. Run-down; but none the worse for that; it seems, given back to itself, somehow.'

'Isn't it – difficult? The Syrian army?'

'I have a friend who lives in the town. I can get the necessary papers.' Strange, how easy I find it to lie to her although I know, inside myself, somewhere very deep, that I am drawn to her in a way I have never experienced before.

'I'd like to do that,' she said. 'Baalbek, the Beka'a Valley! I haven't been there for years. We had a summer house up there once. Once upon a time ...'

Eight

Ramadan Saad – just come in from work, summoned by Abu Hamad personally – sat upright in his chair, watching his leader cautiously: the boss a different man these days … And it seems I am, also? – but he pushed that thought aside as though it were a disloyalty.

The third man in the office at the rear of the FFP safe-house they were in sat a little apart from the other two: a young man, his demeanour self-contained but confident. This was the first time Saad had met him and he had been introduced simply as 'Fahal'. Fahal was observant of his two superiors, aware that there existed between them a closeness from which he was excluded, that blood-and-soul closeness forged during the battles of the early days; he knew himself to be a 'new boy' in their eyes, and was determined to prove himself worthy of their regard, for Abu Hamad's recognition of a man was a pre-requisite to advancement above the mass of rank-and-file henchmen.

' … I've had them keep at the girl but she sticks to her story that she was looking down as he passed by her so she didn't see his face.' Abu Hamad pacing the floor, head bent, hands clasped behind his back. 'Fools!' The word cast at the entire alien world out of his personal anguish. 'They understand nothing!'

'She is very young.' Inside himself Saad still held that even in furtherance of the Cause women – children – should never be heavily menaced, or abused either physically or mentally (a tenet of behaviour he knew Abu Hamad himself had lived by in those early days when they had fought side by side, but had abandoned bit by bit as the advantages to be gained by a more permissive attitude in such matters became apparent to him). But he kept his protest mild, for since the slaying of his daughter Abu Hamad was a driven man. Always ruthless in the prosecution of the Cause, he had become since that act obsessed by a desire for revenge. 'Obsessed'?: Saad considered the word; and judged it fair.

Abu Hamad swung round, stood close to Saad, in front of him. His face was set and there was nothing in his eyes but implacable hatred. But he spoke quietly.

'Someone is going to die for Hessa's death,' he said.

Saad knew it for a vow the man had made to himself. He allowed a small silence of respect for it; and then sought to assuage the bitterness consuming his leader.

'We have the hostages,' he pointed out. 'In time, AKAL will have to succumb; in order to secure the release of those men they will inform us of the identity of the commander within their ranks who ordered the operation. You will have him then. It may take time, but *you will have him.*' The bastard would be wise to kill himself before that happened.

Abu Hamad stared at him grimly. 'I see you have not heard the news,' he said. 'AKAL have seized Mansoor! They seek thus to undermine our position of strength and deny me that which I seek. Legitimately seek, *she was of my blood!* … Well, they will learn.'

Saad was shocked to the core of his being: the actual

abduction of the FFP's father-figure, now made known to him for the first time, that was bad enough, demonstrating as it did a brutal escalation in the seriousness of the confrontation; but Abu Hamad's reaction to it filled him with foreboding.

'But – Ahmed Al Jaffer Mansoor!' He kept his voice low, by an act of will. 'If *he* is in the hands of AKAL, we will have to accept whatever terms they put forward. Have to! Our men will not allow –'

'No, my friend.' Abu Hamad laid special emphasis on "friend", his voice quiet, wrapping the word round with the strong stuff of past comradeship sealed in battle. 'I am blessed in that I have many like you in our Group. *My* will shall prevail. And it is my will that I be given the name of the man who planned for my death – and thus brought about that of my daughter.' He paused; then stated his position in the affair.

'There is only one offer on the table between us and AKAL,' he said harshly. 'They give me the name of that commander of theirs; or our prisoners die. All eight of them.'

'If that happens, they will kill Mansoor, and –'

'That is in the hands of God. But I will never give up until I have the man I seek for Hessa.'

He will start a bloodletting – not for the Cause, but for his own personal revenge: Saad perceived this clearly. And said, nothing.

After a moment, Abu Hamad crossed the room and sat down behind the desk angled across one corner.

'Now to the other point of my summoning you both,' he said, folding his arms. 'The surveillance on the Fanous apartment has revealed that AKAL are in touch with the wife. We may therefore assume that she also is one of their members. We shall now move against her and those about her in a more positive manner. Assessing the situation there according to observed time-patterns of the three occupants, it appears certain that the apartment will be empty between the hours of 17.00 and 19.30 today. This is what I want done ...'

Plans were laid, Saad and Fahal to work together during the course of the projected action. When they were complete, Fahal was ordered to leave, to make specific preparations; Saad was invited to stay on for a while.

'It is good to work with an old friend,' Abu Hamad observed. 'A man who fought side by side with me in the rough days. Today such men are still the heart of my strength, for we *understand* each other. And accept whatever that understanding reveals ...'

Saad left the safe-house half an hour later. And walking the streets of the city – one of which he'd fought his way along house by shattered house in '75, its ruins still desolate these fifteen years on, too many men had died there and people's memories are long and cruel, they stifle at birth any urge to re-build – he thought about Abu Hamad, fellow fighter then, The Boss now. Painfully, he admitted to himself that he no longer truly identified with Abu Hamad. But he was entirely certain that, nevertheless, he would always and swiftly respond to any call-to-arms from him; and that to him alone belonged forever the absolute loyalty, that with-you-to-the-death fealty of himself, Ramadan Saad.

Twelve days of captivity had not scratched the surface of Soheil Fanous' intellectual arrogance, his conviction that in the end he would be the one to triumph; but he continued to conduct himself circumspectly when in the presence of his captors, particularly in that of his interrogator, knowledge of whose name he had requested but been denied. His treatment so far had been harsh, but adequate considering the circumstances: sufficient food and water, that was the most important thing, together with the facts that his concrete cell was dry, no lice infested the two blankets on his bed, and there were no rats, thank God, no rats in the night ...

But time hung heavy. He looked at his watch (restored to him when asked for) and it showed ten o'clock, morning of course, he'd watched night-darkness fade, that one small grimy window allowing him a grey dawn, then his breakfast of khobs and water had been thrust in at the door, the empty tin plate and mug removed a short time later ... He stretched himself out on the bed and closed his eyes. The mind active, however, planning future revenges on behalf of those who because Soheil Fanous was held hostage were being denied the blessings flowing from his skilled hands ... But better those individuals for the present bereft and me safe, he thought (a slight smile lengthening his lips); for – apart from other considerations! – countless sufferers would be the losers in the future were I at this time unable to –

The metal door was flung open, slammed back against the wall with a crash as three men surged into the room. One kicked the door shut again then stood clear, watching, waiting his turn. Fanous had jerked himself upright but the two were already on him, seized his arms and yanked him off the bed, then hauled him across the room and stood him up against the wall. The third joined in then, driving his fist into Fanous' stomach, kneeing him as he bent double over the pain. He fell to the floor. But he knew what he was in for now

– knew also that three to one left him no hope of avoiding physical pain and that therefore he must concentrate on fundamentals. So he closed his will against the instinct to resist, choked it to death. And took his beating with disciplined and punishing passivity, using his body with one goal and one only: *to protect, to keep safe from injury his eyes and hands*. Damage to either might mean he would never operate again.

... They left him on the floor. After a time he dragged himself across to the bucket and vomited into it. Then crawled to the bed and slowly and painfully arranged his body upon it, lying on his back, head resting on the lumpy pillow. When his breathing had quietened, lifted both his hands up in front of his face, palms inward; and examined them minutely, flexing each finger individually, then turning them so that he could inspect their backs. On being satisfied that they had suffered no permanent damage, he lowered them again, spreading them on the blanket, enjoying their continued ability to sense its roughness. Closed his eyes at last; and let the near-sleep of exhaustion possess him ...

The opening of the door brought him awake instantly. He knew a moment's fear but then the man standing beside the bed spoke to him quietly and he was a stranger, not one of the four jailers known to him.

'I will take you to the interrogator,' he said.

As he was led along that now-familiar way, Fanous conned over the possible motives behind his beating. But none that came to mind seemed to make any sort of sense, and by the time he was sitting facing his enemy across the teak desk he had come to the conclusion that there was something in what had just taken place that did not fit into the scheme of things as at present known to him. There must have been some new development, he reasoned; and resolved to deal with his interlocutor cunningly and with restraint – though anger was boiling inside him, he longed to lash out at someone, anyone, in payment for his own present suffering and degradation – in the hope of discovering what that new development might be.

But no cunning proved necessary. What he sought was given him almost immediately, and with minimal effort on his part.

'I regret that you have been beaten.' The interrogator sitting stiffly in his chair, and his manner formal.

'Why was it done?' Hold the rage back – find out, first.

'An FFP man has been abducted by AKAL.'

'So why beat *me*?'

'The man taken was Mansoor, Ahmed Al Jaffer Mansoor. When I heard of this outrage, I lost control. For his sake I wanted blood to flow – enemy blood, any enemy, and you were to my hand.'

Fanous drew a deep breath. A new situation, indeed. Ahmed Al Jaffer Mansoor, the 'father' of the FFP, no less; an old man now, widely revered, deeply meshed into the FFP hierarchy through marriages and family and still having an authoritative say in Group affairs … If it was really true that AKAL had Mansoor then the position of himself, Soheil Fanous, was indeed drastically altered – provided the game was played a certain way.

'So why do you regret my beating now?' Fanous had pushed his anger to the back of his mind; was seeking properly to understand how things stood so that he might take to himself any advantage available, or at least be ready to do so should the opportunity arise.

The interrogator shifted in his chair. And now sought

to ensure his own personal safety in the future, should Fanous be returned safely to the world, by assuaging his prisoner's present physical discomfort and, doubtless (though it was being kept well hidden), his anger. Released hostages, he knew, had a habit of repaying in full measure any punishment they themselves had suffered while held captive; many such cases he knew of –

'I reproach myself for ordering it.' Violent memories of one such "repayment" caused his apology to run swiftly off his tongue. 'I was too hasty. I allowed my high regard for Al Jaffer Mansoor to influence me … I have given orders that when you are returned to your cell here, a doctor will attend you; and after that, a good meal will be provided …'

Two hours later, his cuts and bruises cleansed and treated with ointments and a good meal of mutton stew and rice inside him, Fanous considered the information he had acquired. So – if his interrogator were to be believed, and everything pointed to his having spoken the truth – AKAL had reacted at last. And boldly – or foolhardily? It had been known for the sort of tit-for-tat hostage-taking they had apparently now embarked on to end up militating against the real interests of the very hostage(s) it had been designed to help: sometimes stalemate was reached and all those held were 'put on ice', maybe for years, while the executive body of each side turned its attention to more pressing or more promising activities; and sometimes patience snapped, a killing ensued and was swiftly followed by chain-reaction killings, the objective of the original 'strike' lost beneath a surge of mutual viciousness …

Well, it was done now; a new piece had been brought into play. The FFP now held himself, Soheil Fanous, together with seven run-of-the-mill AKAL auxiliaries; AKAL held one man only but (since FFP were still ignorant of the potential value to them of Soheil Fanous) that man well chosen. Mansoor, patriarch of the FFP, a fierce and steadfast old man, unremitting and pitiless in his prosecution of the Fundamentalist cause! With him their prisoner, AKAL were in a strong bargaining position: in return for his safe freedom, they could demand – they could confidently demand – the freeing of *all* their men held by the FFP; and in all probability even Abu Hamad would not dare to stand out against such a deal by insisting that it include the naming of the man responsible (albeit unintentionally, bigger game had been the target!) for the death of that girl of his? Abu Hamad would surely reason that were he to attempt that, there existed a strong possibility that *he* would be the one forced in the end to back down – would realize, too, that he stood to lose more than just the argument, after that!

The trade now on offer: Mansoor, in return for eight AKAL men, none of whom was considered by the FFP to be of any particular standing within his Group, and one of whom was Soheil Fanous … Clean and well fed in his cell, Fanous smiled, licking his swollen lips: Mansoor the real prize (at least, seen to be so by those possessed of limited information!), so AKAL could afford to laugh in the face of the FFP should they try to hold out for the name of the man Abu Hamad doubtless intended to hunt to the death in revenge for the killing of his daughter …

'How's Tagarid bearing up, now time's gone on a bit?' Geraldine was stacking her books away in her locker in the staffroom, and spoke over her shoulder to Lois who was sitting at the central table, lighting a cigarette. 'She's not too destroyed?'

Lois inhaled, put the spent match in an ashtray. She was not quite sure of the answer to that question, and felt that Geraldine deserved the truth – at least whatever she considered to be the truth. Finally:

'I'm seeing a side of her I didn't know was there,' she said.

Geraldine turned and came over; saw her staring moodily down at the glowing tip of the cigarette in her hand. 'Tell me?' she suggested.

'I'd have expected she would be, like you said, destroyed.' Head still bent, the dark auburn hair gleaming. 'Well, she doesn't seem to be ... I should be glad she isn't, I suppose. But it makes me feel ... I don't know. I don't understand.'

Geraldine reached out impulsively, laid a hand on her forearm. 'Too many negatives by half,' she said. 'Let's be positive. *Not* destroyed, that's good, surely. Then – how is she?'

'Angry.' It came out at once; Lois looked up as she said it and there was a small smile on her lips and a lively curiosity in her eyes. 'I've hardly ever known Tagarid to be visibly angry about anything before, she's not a "hot" sort of person ... Oddly enough, I like her better for it.'

'When I came in, though, I thought you looked depressed?'

Lois shook her head. 'No. Just thinking. You see I don't really know who the anger is directed against.' Getting to her feet, she stubbed the half-smoked cigarette out in the ashtray. 'Time I was going –'

'Give you a lift? It's not much out of my way.'

The offer was readily accepted. Together they went down to the Renault and drove off. Geraldine was a very careful driver and knew the city well; as they slowly progressed through the lit streets towards Caracole el Druze:

'How's Fahal Rizik getting on?' she asked, for he had been a favourite student with her, being both intelligent and hardworking, a pleasure to teach.

'He wasn't in class this evening. First time he's missed since I took over from you.'

'Maybe something to do with the clearance for the Saudi job. Those offices are a nightmare, they say you have to more or less camp there to be sure of your turn ... I saw him the other day.'

'At the Academy?'

'No. He came to my place, to see Nizar. They're friends. They've known each other for quite a while.'

Lois sat quiet while a crossroads was negotiated. Then asked a question that had become possible between the two of them by this time, they having moved easily into a closeness welcomed by both since each was in some sense lonely, was hungry for congenial companionship uncomplicated by any lasting commitment on either side.

When the crossroads lay behind them:

'Geraldine,' she said. 'You're serious about Nizar?'

'Marriage, you mean?' The fair girl paused; and when she went on her voice was self-consciously light, dismissive almost, as if she sought to dance free of any profound personal engagement in the matter – yet also, it seemed to Lois, wished *to be perceived* to be doing so.

'Not really,' she said. 'We're fond of each other, we like being together.' And then after a moment's silence spoke again – but incisively now, all fragile pretending eaten up by passion: 'Like making love together,' she said.

Lois sensed a bitterness in her. Said: 'You're English, he's Syrian, yes ... I've always thought one of the things to live by when you're in love is that old old precept, "to thine own self be true". *Both* the lovers; and each to be honest with the other about it, no dissimulation *for any reason whatsoever.*'

The Renault proceeded in its customary deliberate fashion. After a moment Geraldine said quietly, 'I could never live the life of a wife to an officer in the Syrian army. I've thought about it and I know it's not possible for me. But take that career away from him, and he is nothing ... Suppose we went to Britain, what could he do, there? Answer, inescapably, nothing likely to be meaningful to him ... So, we make love a lot; and *live* together.' She pulled the car in beside the kerb, slid the gear-change into neutral. Drew a deep breath, then leaned back in her seat, staring out through the windscreen at the street revealed in the headlights. 'We've arrived,' she observed flatly.

Lois didn't move. 'I like knowing you,' she said.

A small silence; then Geraldine faced her, making a smile with her mouth but her eyes sombre. 'Come round for a drink, my place, Saturday evening?' she invited.

'Will Nizar be there?'

She nodded. 'Of course.'

Lois accepted; then thanked her for the lift and got out. As the Renault drove away, she crossed the courtyard and entered the apartment block. In the lift, looked at her watch: 8.15, so she would be the first home, Tagarid seldom got home before 8.20, and this night, Wednesday, was Liliane's disco evening, she wouldn't be in until 9.30, at which time they would all have supper together ...

She let herself in with her keys: two locks on the door, but the outer flexed steel gates were never closed until 10 o'clock so she did not carry the key to their padlock; two of them there were, one in Tagarid's keeping and the other held by Salaam, best for an 'outside' person to have means of access should some emergency arise … Hanging up her jacket in the hall, she opened the door to go into the lounge, and –

Gasped. Stood frozen for a second and then stepped forward into the room. Slowly. Her head turning from side to side as she peered in shock and horror at the appalling ruin of this living-room in her sister's home (and the air of it reeking of liquor). Bar cabinet smashed open, broken glass and spilt booze fouling the carpet; cushions slashed, their innards spilling out like guts out of ripped abdomens; pictures and lampshades cut to pieces, they must have used razors –

Thank God none of us was here! The relief of it stopped her in her tracks. She stood still amidst the chaos and gathered herself together. Looked around again, this time with slow deliberation, forcing herself to take it all in, facing down the brute nastiness of it … *It is obscene*, she thought. Found herself trembling (knew that for rage, not fear) and finding an unbroken glass and a bottle of brandy – airline stuff, she'd brought it in herself and tucked it away at the back of the cabinet – poured out a stiff measure and drank it down.

Then, bracing herself for more to come, went round the rest of the apartment. Saw that although all the other rooms had obviously been entered, they had suffered little real damage: bedspreads dragged off, drawers opened and their contents scattered, clothes pulled out of wardrobes and tossed about – the intention simply to create a mess, not to destroy, in the other rooms.

Returning to the sitting-room, she poured herself a second brandy, smaller than the first, carried it into the kitchen (no 'spoiling' done there, which was a great relief) and sipped it slowly but regularly while she brewed coffee and set a tray with cups and saucers, milk and sugar. Leaving the coffee on the hob she carried the tray into the lounge and set it down on the central table (that polished surface hideously scarred now, by knives viciously used); found two more clean and unbroken glasses and placed them, together with the bottle of brandy, beside it; and as she did so, heard the key turn in the lock of the front door.

Tagarid, come home.

They had checked through the apartment and found that only two things were missing: a high-grade portable radio, taken from the lounge; and a thick gold chain carrying a pendant which Lois had left lying on the dressing-table in her bedroom. The pendant was very precious to her, for it had been willed to her by her father: it had come from Baalbek, he had bought it there in '68 as a present for his wife, mother to their two small girls. It held clasped in a circlet of beaten gold a scarab of dark green malachite upon which was engraved a verse from the Quran, the script archaic, the workmanship very fine ... Nothing else had been taken, although there had been other jewellery to be had, and various expensive electronic equipment.

'They seek to frighten us.' Tagarid on her second brandy. 'But *why?*'

'Softening us up.' Liliane; she was shivering but had refused brandy and would not go to bed. 'They want something from one of us –'

The phone rang. 'I'll take it,' Lois said. Crossed the

room and lifted the receiver.

'Next time we shall call when someone's in.' Man's voice in her ear; expressionless, bored even. 'Perhaps it will be Liliane ... Yes, Liliane; and alone ...'

The phone went dead. Lois had turned her back to the others; and now said into the receiver, quietly but with a suitable touch of impatience, 'No I'm sorry there's no-one of that name here, you must have the wrong number.'

Nine

The 'Dolphin Club' was a pleasant place, its aquamarine swimming pool surrounded by an area of lilac tiling, and that ringed beyond by gardens; its changing rooms, leisure-rooms and a domed cool restaurant were spaced out amidst more gardens and arbours, and the entire complex was hedged in from the outside world with tall evergreens tended and clipped to impenetrable perfection. Membership was costly, for it was luxuriously appointed, having been built twenty-five years earlier when Beirut was still the playground of the Arab world.

Nowadays, those who used it did not flaunt their wealth; but it had no lack of members.

Tagarid and Lois – one-piece suits still damp from a swim in the pool – lay on sunbeds placed beneath a lilac-and-white awning, for it was midday and the sun high in a cloudless sky. They had been busy at the apartment until 11 o'clock – Lois having telephoned Leila and begged the morning off, reporting to her the disaster of the previous evening – and then had left Salaam in charge of things. A firm of decorators had been at work there since 8 a.m., and Tagarid had placed various orders by phone; replacement furnishings and so on would be arriving from time to time …

'Clean, now.' Tagarid spoke softly, lying back, her eyes closed. 'All that – that *filth* – washed out of me. All my hatred of it, too … For the moment.'

Lois said nothing; but she sat up and glanced at her sister.

'*My home.*' The voice hardening. 'It's as if some enemy had gone *rutting* in there.'

'But who was it?' Lois had turned away, was staring at the blue-green lure of the water; and went on persuasively. 'Move clear of the beastliness of it now; *move on* – there's something here we need to think about.'

After a moment: 'What? What else is there?'

'For one thing – how did they get in?'

'We went over that last night. Had the locks changed this morning.'

'Have you thought about – Salaam?'

That penetrated the skin. Tagarid's eyes flicked open; she lay tense, frowning. Then: 'Never,' she said. 'She'd never *do that* to me.'

'What makes you so certain?'

'I *know* her. She's decent, loyal.'

'Loyal?' Lois seized on the word; and sought to pin-point its immediate relevance, saying, 'Maybe she is. But, to whom does her loyalty belong? Ultimately?' Thoughtfully, she developed her argument. 'She is Syrian. The Syrians are playing a devious hand in the Lebanon. And there would be all sorts of persuasions they could apply, the crack of the whip, the dangling carrot –'

'No! She and I, we get on well together, always have. We *like* each other. I'd not have been fool enough to give her the keys in the first place unless I felt sure of her.'

'Will you give her the new ones?'

'I will.' Stubbornly rejecting the concept of so personal a betrayal. '*And* I'll leave in her hands the emergency key to the outer steel gate. Someone's got to have it, obviously, lest one of these days I lose or forget mine; otherwise I'd have to call the fire brigade to get in.'

Salaam? And Fahal Rizik? And – but where do you call a halt to the fearful shadowy wonderings? 'Can anyone trust anyone in this city these days?' Lois' voice brooding; her eyes on the flowers (but at the moment they don't stand a chance of getting inside her and blooming there). 'Beirut. The feel of it gets worse. Even just in the year since I was last here. Violence is winning out. Fifteen years of it: people are exhausted, they're drawing back into the small separateness of themselves; there's a dreadful sense of the framework of society – like the city itself – crumbling away. The never-ending tension, the bombardments, beginning finally to destroy foundations, what little coherence there was left …'

'You're getting carried away.' Determinedly, Tagarid essayed humour: 'It's working in that publishing-house, you're becoming fanciful, playing with words,' she said. And closed her eyes again, lifting one arm and pillowing her head on it. After a moment added softly, 'Those who've left Lebanon, gone to sweeter places, they play with words. But we who stay on, we play with – other things.'

Two teenaged girls swept out of the changing-rooms, ran lissom-light across the lilac tiling and dived into the pool. Lois saw the surface of the blue water shatter into vortexed ripples and white flying spray …

'Lois.'

'Yes?' She turned her head and saw her sister sitting

up on her sunbed, regarding her intently, arms clasped about her knees: the long dark hair loose and flowing below her shoulders. Oh but she is lovely, Lois thought –

'I lied to you.' Tagarid's eyes unblinking; she spoke softly, making her confession. 'On the phone, when I called you in England, I lied; and ever since then I've been living out that lie. I want to stop now.'

Lois slipped down to sit on the lilac tiling, closer to her.

'So tell me,' she said, her eyes on the two girls now racing each other through the water.

'I had been planning to leave Soheil, you see,' the level voice went on at once. 'To go to California, to our cousins there. It was all arranged, plane tickets and so on – and a job waiting for me, a company Uncle Louis is director of ... a new life, as they say.' Self-mockery giving edge to the last words.

Forbidding herself to look at her sister – (Don't touch her, don't breach her tight self-control, don't react too strongly: do any of those and she'll break apart.) – Lois fought to a standstill the confusion in her own mind. And then made a statement she'd always assumed to be true, but questioning it now by the tone of her voice. 'You love him?'

'Oh yes. But he doesn't love me. These last years he's barely "seen" me ... I'm good to look at, I'm satisfactory in bed, I'm a competent housekeeper and I'm doing a useful job in our broken city: for these things, he likes me, and besides that it suits him. But love, no ... The capacity for love: I think Soheil has sublimated his to the service of his skills.'

'You didn't – talk to him about how you felt?'

A shake of the head. 'No. I knew he wouldn't want to

lose me – lose my various services, let's be honest – and I'm not strong enough to stand against him. I knew he would have talked me back to him … That's why I decided I must leave Lebanon: because if I stayed he would always be able to call me back. Always, I'd have returned if he asked.'

For Lois, the pieces were tumbling into place. 'And you wanted me to be here to keep things going for Soheil and Liliane while they adjusted to the fact you'd gone.' It came out harshly, she couldn't help it: the realization of being 'used' never easy to take.

Tagarid put her hands out towards her in a familiar gesture of hers in moments of emotional stress, a quick, nervous giving-yet-entreating.

'It would only have been for a little while, a week at most, if things had gone straightforwardly,' she said. 'And I knew you would come. You've always been my sheet-anchor when I needed one.'

Turning to her, Lois caught her hands, pressed them. 'You, mine. Over the years.' Smiled suddenly, briefly. 'Not so often, though,' she added.

But it glanced unnoticed off the hard surface of Tagarid's preoccupation. 'But Soheil was kidnapped,' she went on. 'I couldn't go, then. Can't, until he's freed or – until I *know*.'

'That could take a long time?'

She frowned. 'Hopefully, not. I think it will all be resolved soon. It has to be tied in together in some way, all that's been happening, that AKAL man coming to see me, the FFP leader Mansoor –'

'Do you think – now – it's possible that Soheil is actually *part of it*?'

'Involved, you mean? In Group politics, terrorism?' She shook her head vehemently. 'No! I can't believe that.

Someone's made a mistake.'

Lois saw her sister's face, her entire body, tense up in rejection; and she moved away from it quickly, asking:

'Why, suddenly *today* you tell me about leaving him? I've been here nearly two weeks –'

'Because of last night. And again because of a few minutes ago, what you were saying about trusting people ... It made me want to be properly honest with you. You see there's only you, really. I've got to level with *one* person.'

'So what will you do? Will you go to the States – eventually?'

'I'm no longer as sure as I was.'

'You've got to decide –'

'Stop! Look, please leave it. Let things go on as they are, for the time being. When Soheil is free again – I think I'll know then whether to go, or stay with him ... It seems to me possible that he may be changed, himself, by what's happening. Maybe he will *value me* again.'

Suddenly aware of how much time had gone by, Lois scrambled to her feet. 'I must go home and have some lunch or I'll be late for afternoon class,' she said, gathering together her towel and beach-bag.

'Lois!' The voice high and sharp. 'That phone call last night, the one you took soon after I got back. Was it really a wrong number?'

Towel and bag clasped in her arms, Lois straightened slowly, looking sidelong into her sister's eyes.

'No,' she admitted. 'Since we've decided to live in mutual honesty with each other, *no it was not a wrong number*. It was a man. He said, "Next time we'll call when someone's in. Perhaps it will be Liliane, and alone". He terminated the call, then ...' She turned away, stood looking at the sun-glazed water of the pool. 'Those were his exact words,' she murmured. 'Funny, remembering them so clearly when what you'd really like is to forget.'

Swift movement behind her, then Tagarid standing at her side, touching her shoulder lightly with one hand, establishing a brief physical unity.

'I'm afraid.' Her voice low and unsteady. 'For the first time since all this began, I'm truly afraid.'

'If Soheil is as you say entirely – innocent, if that's the word? I mean if he is *in* this situation but not *of* it – then surely you have nothing to fear? There's no way for you to be, as it were, important to either of the warring sides, they've *no reason* to strike at you and yours?'

No answer.

'Tarri?'

Quietly: 'Whatever else he may have failed me in, he would never fail me in that. It would entail deceiving me, *in his heart*. That's – not possible.'

Lois kissed her on the cheek. Then, deliberately casual, 'See you this evening,' she said. 'I won't forget the chocolates – I'll call in at "Moustafa's" on the way home.'

Later, walking quickly along the sunlit pavements on her way to the Academy, she thought about Soheil. A man known to her for over six years now but that 'knowing' relatively superficial: a complicated man, and highly gifted; physically attractive; and an arrogance to him ... Then, for the first time, it came to her mind that there was perhaps a certain inconsistency in the premise that a man such as Soheil Fanous should stand aside from the internecine warfare which for the last fifteen years had been slowly but very surely ripping apart the once-beautiful fabric of his native land and now looked close to putting in hand its final dissolution; that he should find it in himself meekly to stand aside and – merely *watch that being done*?

... Suppose Soheil actually *was* part of the involved and vicious struggle for power euphemistically referred to by most citizens as 'The Events'? That would open up a whole new ball-game – no, that would open the gates into a truly dreadful world: *terrorism, and all that therein is* –

Grimly, she slammed the doors of her mind against any such possibility. And launched herself vigorously into the living of the day (but during it realized sometimes that she was laughing too much, too easily – and recognized it for that determined laughter used to mask a new and frightening uncertainty).

Sunday dawned clear and bright. By 10 o'clock she and Fahal were on their way to Baalbek, Fahal's borrowed Honda running the narrow streets of out-of-town Beirut smoothly – he was a good driver – then taking on the long climb towards the heights of Mount Lebanon ... Over the top, and down to Shtaura (and don't even look at that restaurant, Fahal will drive you on past it and you can remember it from the safety of your car – even spit on it, in your mind, if you damn well want to!) ... Through to Zahlé (where 'they' seized Soheil *and where in God's name is he now?* – no, put that aside also for this one day, agonizing over it solves nothing, merely advances your own gradual dissolution). Then the great swathe of fertile land opening out in front of you, the Beka'a Valley, narrow at first as you come down into it from the hills but soon to broaden, ten miles wide it is as you approach Baalbek where the Romans built their awesome complex of temples, seeking to demonstrate in stone the permanence of their (long-lost) hegemony ...

'I thought we might eat our picnic lunch at Yamouné.' Fahal broke the silence that had grown between them over the last several miles. 'Would you like that?'

'We never went there, we always stayed this side of the Valley.' She turned to him, smiling. 'Why not? You know it well?'

'Years ago.'

He was in profile to her and she did not observe the narrowing of his eyes. 'I've heard it said the place is a centre for the trade in hash,' she remarked, looking out once more at the road ahead. 'Is it?'

'They say ... But it is also very beautiful. And its Roman past more private nowadays from – visitors.'

The slight hesitation informed her of his quick decision to blur the issue, to escape it if he could. She returned him to it.

'You mean people who don't "belong", I think,' she said. 'But doesn't that include someone like me? Only half-Lebanese, and choosing to live elsewhere?'

He did not make a direct answer. 'It must be strange, knowing you "relate" to two countries. Are somehow divided into two separate and entirely different parts ... The tensions of choice ...' Abruptly, he gave a short laugh; then glanced across at her. 'So we go to Yamouné?' he asked, his tone light now, and an eagerness in it. 'I want very much to show you, to be there with you.'

'Yamouné it is.' She was glad he had not pursued his previous line of thought; yet had a feeling he would return to it eventually, maybe not this day even, but – some other time. It occurred to her that she hoped he would. Why hope that, she asked herself then? But wasn't sure she liked the answer, which was: because he is beginning *to matter* to you ...

He turned the Honda left off the highway and they began working their way in among the foothills, the road traversing the slopes in long slow curves, quite narrow but its surface good, not continually harrowed by military traffic as was the main road. And quiet; they saw no other vehicle until they drove into the haphazard streets of the little town.

A little town tucked in at the foot of a steep south-facing scarp; its rich villas widely spaced, their gardens lush with trees and flowering shrubs, its lesser dwellings built cheek-by-jowl but neat and clean. Sunlight pouring down and not a soul to be seen. A small breeze ruffling blossom in the gardens.

Fahal drove through to the southern outskirts and parked the car in a large open space backed onto by a row of barns. They got out and stretched, easing the stiffness out of their bodies.

'Where *is* everyone?' she asked. And answered herself, 'The mums indoors, dads at work, children in school, I suppose.' Stood looking around her, smoothing creases out of her blouse and jeans.

'The big villas are owned mostly by those hash-barons you spoke of.' Fahal had gone to the rear of the car and was opening the boot. 'They install caretakers, come here only in the summer … Let's have a drink, then climb up to the pool. I'll carry the picnic, and we'll eat up there.'

The bottled water was ice-cold from the cooler-box: they drank, and laughed together with the pleasure of it after the dusty heat of the drive, their eyes dazzled by sunshine.

'The "pool"? Where's that?' she asked, standing with her back to the rocky cliffs towering above the town.

He pointed high up behind her, to the left; and she turned, looking up. Some distance from where they stood the scarp rose steeply, its ridged summit 500 feet above them, etched against blue sky: and just below that summit, saw water gushing out, pouring out of apparently solid rock to rush on down the cliff-face, a deep ravine it had carved for itself, eroding to bedrock and the water tumbling down in a series of 'steps', white water all the way ... The sun shining directly upon it ...

She gazed, enthralled. Fahal watched her face.

When she turned to him again, he looked away.

'The pool's up there?' Her voice quiet.

He nodded, lifting the picnic haversack out of the boot. 'Artesian spring,' he remarked. 'Wonders of nature – it's a stiff climb,' he added. 'Sure you want to?'

She smiled at him and said nothing; then reached in through the open car door for her hat; it was a floppy-brimmed affair of khaki drill and she put it on, adjusting the brim to shade her eyes.

As they walked towards the place where the fall reached level ground, they passed, skirting its edges, a large circular area lush wih rank grass and bushes, yellow water-irises massed among the green, its boundaries marked by pollarded willows.

'When the Romans lived here that was a small lake,' Fahal told her, nodding towards it. 'They were a people who made good use of natural resources ... And rendered proper thanks to God for them,' he added quietly.

'In what way? How d'you mean?'

'You will see.' He grinned across at her. 'Have to climb to the top to do so, though.'

Fahal leading, they worked their way upwards, keeping close in beside the water, traces of a footpath to guide them. Rough terrain: arid gritty ground studded with boulders, sometimes treacherous with scree, the feet having to seek out firm purchase, slipping often then finding bruising stone to halt the slide, and the hands grazed as they grabbed for safe-hold. The roar of the water enclosing all other sound, and the air filled with fine spray. Sun beating down on the back, sweat trickling into the eyes –

Ahead of her, Fahal halted suddenly, staring down at something below him and to his left. Climbing up beside him, breathing hard, she followed the direction of his gaze. Saw, close in under the lip of the ravine, a small grassy hollow; and stretched out at his ease within it, a youth, asleep. He lay on his back, left arm flung out to the side, the right up over his face shielding his eyes from the sun; he was dressed in shirt and jeans, and his feet were bare. Near his shoulder lay an open book.

'Playing hookey from school.' She murmured the words, smiling. 'And what a place to do it in. One's own and very private refuge.' But then she looked at Fahal. Beside her, close, his face was dark and shut, his mouth tight as he stared unblinking at the boy lying asleep in the sun; and she knew he was at that moment living in some other place. Knew too that wherever and whatever that place was, it was sunless.

She shivered. And moving as quietly as she could, climbed on, up the steep meandering trail. Not to disturb the boy, for surely it would be horrible – frightening – to come awake and discover one's sleeping undefended self had been exposed to the inquisitive eyes of strangers. That was the reason she gave herself to account for her sudden urgent desire to withdraw unnoticed; but she knew that what had in fact powered that desire was her need to escape from a Fahal abruptly and differently perceived, a man infinitely 'older', hard and secret ...

When next she stopped to rest, to wipe sweat off her face, draw breath, and gaze about her at the wonderful vista now spread out before her eyes from the new and higher viewpoint, Fahal caught up with her and halted at her side.

'Is it worth the climb?' he asked.

'Every drop of sweat, every blister, every pint of Dettol I shall use tonight.'

'Let's get on then. None of that will matter once you've seen the pool.'

It was true. They climbed higher still. And below the tunnel-like cavern in the rock out of which the water poured, held within the shelter of the curving rock-faces winging out to either side of it, lay a miniature lake. The fall entered it at one end, plunging down into it, throwing up spray that glittered in sunlight; and on the opposite side, flowed out, and down. Except for the vortex at the in-fall, the surface of the water was near-smooth and crystal-clear.

She stood, absorbing the 'feel' of this place: an 'otherness' that brushed the skin of self lightly, waiting to see …

'What was there, here?' she asked after a while.

'A temple. The Romans dedicated it to the Goddess of the Spring. It was built over the centre of the pool … If you look carefully you can see shaped stone down there at the bottom.' He pointed.

She looked; and found … then turned to him.

'Was it deliberately destroyed, an act of vengeance by those who wished to annihilate every trace of Roman domination?' she asked. 'Or, being left untended by its creators when they in their turn were overcome, did it simply, over the years, disintegrate of its own accord?'

But he was staring into the pool and answered without looking up.

'Whichever, the result was the same,' he said.

'Ultimately, the only difference is the length of time taken to bring about the same end.'

'But considered from the personal point of view – Roman conqueror, or vassal seething with hatred under foreign oppression – it must be much more satisfying to see it happen, to be part of making it happen, in your own lifetime?'

Fahal looked up, then. His eyes met hers but she could not read their expression. After a moment:

'I'm sure you're right,' he said. And then laughed and reached out and took her hand, saying, 'Aren't you hungry? I am. There's a place with some shade over there …'

On a narrow 'shelf' some distance from the pool, stunted but leafy trees gave welcome: and there they ate savoury filafil and cold roast chicken, salad and cheese; drank sweet tea from a thermos flask.

'Fahal,' she said, 'what were you thinking about, when we saw that boy asleep? It made me feel good, seeing him like that, like any schoolboy anywhere in the world when he's got away with being out in the sun instead of shut up in a classroom. I felt like laughing, the sheer fun of it, being young and a bit bad –'

'Nothing particular … But he's a fool, playing truant like that. Stupid.'

She caught the bitterness in his voice. 'I'm sorry,' she said after a moment.

'No.' Staring into his empty cup, twisting it round and round between his fingers, he contradicted himself swiftly. 'In truth, I was thinking of my brother,' he said. 'He's dead. Died when he was about that age. That boy – it reminded me.'

Almost she asked him: how? Refrained; but got her answer nevertheless.

'He was shot dead by a sniper during fighting south of Beirut. Five years ago now.'

'Was he – was he *part of* the fighting?' She had to know.

He looked up at her, his eyes intent on hers. 'He was seventeen and yes, he was part of it ... He was not an impulsive kid throwing stones at people he'd been told were his enemies. *He knew what he was doing.*'

She perceived that he identified proudly with the way his brother had met his death. This saddened her; and then as she considered it more deeply, it aroused certain suspicions in her mind.

'He was not a terrorist,' Fahal said quietly. 'He was a patriot, only that.'

He put it to her without emphasis. Seeking her understanding, it seemed to her – and at once she wanted to *give*, to give him that. Confused, she searched his eyes; discovered there what she desired to see and thrust all suspicion to the back of her mind, seeing no place for it between herself and this man.

She laid a hand on his arm. 'I believe you,' she said, feeling his skin warm beneath her fingers. 'You don't have to argue it to me.' Then withdrew her hand and picked up the flask, shaking it a little. 'There's some left,' she said. 'Pass me your cup and I'll share it out.'

As they made their way back down the track, they discovered the boy had gone: the grassy hollow beside the tumbling water empty now. And then as they drove out of Yamouné they passed several small groups of boys clearly on their way home from school, satchels on the back, strap-bound books under the arm, and once a running tussle in progress, swinging fists and goading onlookers ... The dust raised by the passing of their car swirled up over combatants and supporters alike but it

in no way dampened the ardour of either: as Lois
peered into the rear-view mirror she could see hazed
figures prancing about in unabated fury, fewer
watchers and more fighters now, the battle spreading
wider ...

A short distance out of the town, on a hillside offering
a panoramic view down and along the Beka'a Valley,
Fahal pulled the Honda into a lay-by and switched off.

'Let's get out, and I'll show you something,' he said.
'You can see Baalbek from here, and on a day as clear as
this we'll be able to pick out the trace of the Orontes.'

It was as he said. Standing beside him on the grassed
edge of the lay-by, she looked out over the broad flat
spread of the Valley: in the far distance, the
monumental ruins of the acropolis the Romans had
called the City of the Sun stood out yellow-brown in hot
sunlight, the parched slopes of the Ante-Lebanon
mountains a pale backdrop behind. To the north –

Roaring of car-exhausts smashed into her dreaming
and round the curve of the hill, travelling fast – from
the direction of Yamouné – streamed four saloon-cars.
Dangerously, expertly, they swung into the lay-by and
pulled up with a screaming of tyres, a sudden
cacophony of horns. Startled, unsure, she observed that
the way the cars had been positioned completely boxed
in the Honda.

As if to order, the baying of the horns stopped. Then
the car doors opened and men stepped out onto the
tarmac of the lay-by, stood silently regarding the two
who were strangers to this place. Young men, seven of
them. Dressed in jeans, shirts and jackets: but the
clothes, like the cars, expensive. Some of them were
wearing checkered headcloths, others caps: one alone
was bareheaded, a tall, lithe youth, his black hair

growing thick and curly on his head. It was him you found yourself looking at, Lois thought to herself, without doubt he is the leader of this – gang? She didn't like the word, 'gang'; sinister connotations to it when you're on a remote hillside in Lebanon, unarmed, just the two of you against –

'Salaam aleikum.' The greeting called out by the bareheaded young man broke the silence; and as he spoke, he and all his henchmen moved, fanned out casually to right and left until they stood in a half-circle facing them, barring their way back to the Honda. Then at a sign from the leader, one of them drew a hand-gun from his belt and took up station to one side, levelled his weapon to cover the two thus confronted.

Fahal had returned the man's greeting. Lois said nothing, waiting, head up.

'You came here to buy hash?' The leader spoke loudly, his manner and bearing arrogant, aggressive. 'Which house you buy from?'

'We went to no house.' Fahal answered evenly, standing relaxed but his eyes watchful on the face of his questioner. 'We came here to see the waterfall and the temple-pool –'

'You don't want hash!' Sneering disbelief. 'That is strange to me.' He took three paces forward, stood close in front of Fahal and stared him in the eye. 'People come to Yamouné for hash – ours is the finest in the Valley,' he stated boastfully. 'Deception, that about the pool of the temple,' he went on, menacingly now. 'If you did not come for hash, then it must be that you came to spy on us.'

'Not so!' It burst out of Lois, angrily. 'We came *to see the pool*, and now we're returning –'

He whirled on her, slapped her hard across the face,

and she staggered sideways, crying out involuntarily, arm up to protect herself against further hurt.

'Women have no part in this!' he snapped savagely. 'You keep to your place.' And turned to Fahal again: 'Show me your ID,' he ordered. 'If your papers do not satisfy me, you come with us to be interrogated further. Both of you.'

Slowly, Lois had straightened up: finding no great damage done, no blood on her cheek; and the anger burning brighter now but she had it in check, watching to see what Fahal would do, how he coped with this.

He hadn't moved. 'I see you are a bully as well as a fool,' he said dispassionately to the gang leader, drawing his wallet out of the back pocket of his jeans. From it he extracted a thin red-covered booklet, held it out towards the peremptory hand. 'My papers are in order,' he stated coldly. 'They should suffice to satisfy even you.'

The bareheaded young man snatched it from his hand, began examining the contents of its pages, and of the two loose papers folded within.

And as he did so, Lois saw his face – and then gradually the whole 'look' of him – *change*. The arrogance draining out of him; to leave an overgrown boy suddenly unsure of himself, even a little afraid. Finally, head still down, he meticulously re-folded the papers, then replaced them in the red booklet.

'We'll get the cars out of your way,' he said, holding the booklet out. 'We apologize for detaining you.' Then as Fahal took it from him, he turned his back. 'Get moving!' he called out to his men, waving his arms. 'Let's go!' And as he made for his own car: 'Those two are nothing,' he confided to a nearby comrade – thereby re-establishing his position as leader. 'Waste of time ...'

The four cars reversed and roared off. Lois and Fahal

walked across to the Honda, listening to the silence, looking around at the sunlit hills.

'Makes you realize how lovely peace and quiet can be,' she said, halting by the car, watching Fahal's face as he came up beside her, smiling to him.

'Lois –' But she was already in his arms. Held him tightly and pressed her cheek against his shoulder as he embraced her. They murmured together; not many words spoken but – enough.

And as they drove on towards Baalbek, Lois thought over the matter of those 'papers' Fahal had produced with such instantaneous and extraordinary effect: and came to accept that whatever they might be, they obviously carried clout. In some quarters, or in all, she wondered? And wherein lay their clout? ... She looked at him sideways; and realizing the comparative unimportance of 'papers' at the present time, placed a hand on his knee.

'I'll spell you with the driving whenever you like,' she said as he turned his head to glance at her. Behind the words, her eyes gave him all he wanted from her at that moment. And as they went on to enjoy *that day, together*: 'To this day I give the living thereof,' she whispered to herself. 'No questions, no doubts, no looking forward, no looking back. Just – every moment *to be lived, now.*'

Ten

The FFP leadership held council in a defended-in-depth safe-house in the west of the city: the four top men, each with his chief executive officer beside him, and all seated around a suitably impressive conference table. Coffee and other refreshments were carried in at regular intervals, served to those who desired them; during these interruptions, some occupying no more than a couple of minutes but others more lengthy, discussion was in abeyance; the principals sat absorbed in their own thoughts (often welcoming these opportunities to reassess a personal position either stiffened or abandoned previously) or engaged their field-commanders in whispered conversation. Abu Hamad alone had brought with him no-one of importance. Only Ramadan Saad sat beside him, recalled to active duty as being the one man to be relied on above all others as far as personal loyalty was concerned – because Abu Hamad had come to realize that, in order to manipulate the particular operation presently the subject of review so that his own overriding and highly personal objective (which lay outside its parameters) might yet be achieved, he needed as his right-hand man one bound to him by unbreakable ties of comradeship.

'It's going the way I expected,' he confided to him now as soft drinks went the rounds. 'Nothing I can do about it, though.'

'Once AKAL took Mansoor, the original ploy was doomed.' Saad stating the obvious, and Abu Hamad turned away impatiently, frowning. He was aware that he must now withdraw his opposition to the proposal before the meeting – a futile opposition, he'd suspected that from the beginning, but his craving for revenge had driven him on, causing him to withhold as long as possible his acceptance of the terms put forward by AKAL as the price for their release of the FFP's father-figure. His resistance to it must not be further prolonged, however: already he was effectively isolated as the sole voice standing out against the action necessary to secure Mansoor's freedom, and he knew that for an extremely dangerous position to be in since it could only too easily be exploited by those jealous of his power ...

The servants withdrew. Business was resumed and Abu Hamad spoke at once, stepping into line with his peers.

'The life and liberty of Ahmed Al Jaffer Monsoor is of paramount importance to us all,' he declared, assuming a fine air of benign solemnity (which deceived some of those present, but by no means all). 'Therefore, in this case, we have no alternative but to strike hands with our enemies. I withdraw my objections unreservedly: the eight hostages we seized on 8th May should be handed over, as soon as it may be arranged, in exchange for the release of our founder and mentor.'

They were not surprised by his abrupt change of stance, having known from the outset that in reality he had no choice, not if he wanted to retain his status within the Group; and proceeded without comment to thrashing out in detail their own stipulations to be forwarded to AKAL in regard to the implementation of the exchange of hostages. This was a protracted and difficult task, for each Group would protect most jealously its own 'face' in the matter; and would take every precaution against treachery, both having had it brought home to them many times during the long years of conflict that he who lives by the stab-in-the-back lays himself open to the probability of dying by the same ...

When at last and in his due turn Abu Hamad left the safe-house, Ramadan Saad went with him to his car, saw him into the rear seat, shut the door upon him and then got in behind the wheel, for on this occasion he was acting as his leader's chauffeur. The black Mercedes slid away from the kerb and proceeded on its way, keeping to back streets and shadowed by two jeeps manned by bodyguards.

'We were fools not to anticipate and forestall AKAL's retaliation against Mansoor.' Saad voiced it tentatively. He sensed that Abu Hamad was drum-tight with the anger and frustration within him, and he hoped he might draw him into conversation – and the tension eased then, perhaps, draining out of him like poison from a festering wound. Suppose the boss didn't want to talk, he'd get a stinging rebuff; he knew that but it didn't bother him, if it came he'd set it aside in the name of fraternity, whereas if his remark served its purpose – then good, an old friend aided, a friend so far above him nowadays that it wasn't often he got the chance even to be in his presence, let alone ease the slow burn of vengefulness now consuming him.

A growled assent was all Saad received in answer. The

car travelling smoothly onwards, both men sat in silence.
Until suddenly Abu Hamad sat forward in his place (and
Saad, glancing sideways, saw his face taut and brooding,
his eyes staring out through the windscreen at the road
ahead but clearly not in fact seeing that, other 'pictures'
surely tormenting the eye of his mind).

'This exchange, it doesn't settle anything *for me*,' he
said harshly. 'My daughter was slain deliberately, by the
enemy. *Someone* is going to pay the blood-price for that. If
I cannot get the man I want for it, I *will not* go unpaid. I
will have one death for hers and I will have it soon. One
death in the enemy camp ...'

The FFP in Beirut was putting pressure on AKAL to
move faster in the establishing of the various and
meticulous arrangements necessary to effect the
exchange of hostages agreed between the two Groups:
they had called a strike for the following day, all places of
business and pleasure to remain closed between the
hours of 9 a.m. and 4 p.m. The citizens had learned a
long time ago that it was advisable to obey such calls: the
Group demanding the shut-down would put their bully-
boys on the streets in cars and station-wagons, well-
armed men and in-training boys, with orders to enforce
the strike where necessary, a free hand how you go about
it, fellers, there'll be no questions asked about any
resulting 'trouble', you can count on that ...

Lois found herself unable to remain in bed, however,
though the evening before she had thought it would be
luxury to do just that. But at eight o'clock the sun was
shining into her room and sleep seemed a waste of time
so she got up and dressed; went into the kitchen and
found Tagarid and Liliane already having breakfast.

'Will Salaam be coming in, after four?' Lois making

toast, glanced across at her sister.

Tagarid on her third cup of coffee. She shook her head. 'I said to take the whole day. She's done us cold chicken for lunch. With tabouli. She's put everything ready for us to assemble it.'

'You gave her the new keys?'

'I did. She's got those two and the other, the one to the steel gate. She's always had that ... *I trust her*,' she added, meeting her sister's doubting eyes. 'Salaam's – I feel she's more of a friend to me than most of the people I know these days.'

Sad comment, thought Lois, studying the grave and lovely profile; and was suddenly engulfed in a rush of love for her sister, a desire properly to convey that love, to somehow get it into Tagarid's very being so that it would always be part of her. But carefully, controlled her emotion (always have, haven't I?). And turned to Liliane.

'What do you think of the strike?' she asked. Something to say (to hide behind, perhaps?).

The girl regarded her coolly. Shrugged, pushing her fingers through her curly hair. 'That it steals the living-time of ordinary people. That the Groups – FFP, in this case – arrogate to themselves powers they have no right to exercise.'

Surprised, interested now, Lois sat forward. 'Do a lot of students think as you do?'

'Probably 75 per cent. But nil per cent would admit it.'

'And the other 25? Do they think this kind of strike is a good thing – think it serves a purpose worthy of being served?'

The dark eyes too wary, and frighteningly cynical for sixteen. 'Oh, they're the ones who are active members of one Group or another, so they just do what they're told.'

She got up and began to gather together cups and saucers. 'My current boyfriend is riding with one of the patrols today,' she said. 'Hamra, the morning stint.'

Tagarid stiffened. 'Carrying a gun?'

'Of course, carrying a gun. There wouldn't be much point without one, would there?' She stacked crockery beside the sink, then put on one of Salaam's aprons, saying over her shoulder, 'I'll wash up.'

That done, the tabouli mixed, and everything set ready for lunch, it was still only 11.30. They went into the lounge. Tagarid sat down and began working at her tapestry; Liliane stretched herself out on the floor, gave her attention to a 'set' novel; and Lois – Lois tried to read, but could not settle to it; went to stand by a window and stared out at blue sky and sunshine (but you can't go out there until 4 p.m., can you?) ... Oh hell, why not? –

'I'm going for a walk,' she announced, turning and moving away towards the hall.

'Wiser to say indoors, surely?' Tagarid looked up, her needle stilled.

Liliane said nothing and kept her eyes on her book. But Lois sensed that she was listening and wondered whether she might actually like to accompany her.

'I'll simply be – walking,' she answered quietly. 'It's the places of business they gun for, I won't go anywhere near those.' At the door, she paused, looked back at them, still hoping Liliane might come with her; but the girl's head was down, as if uninterested. Lois laughed. 'It's the English in me,' she said, going on her way out of the room. 'The midday sun calls. To me and other mad dogs.'

But as she slipped on a loose white jacket, she sobered: yes, that probably just about sums up the mental state of anyone abroad on the streets of Beirut this day, she thought. Old songs, new slants to them ...

The city peculiarly emotive to her that morning. The area around the Shams building was deserted; its few little shops all obediently closed, steel shutters down, heavily padlocked; the apartment blocks bereft of their usual lively stir of people going in and out or standing chatting with neighbours ... The broad sweep of Caracole el Druze empty of traffic ... 'The Bridge', that flyover linking Moslem and Christian Beirut, a silent witness to the totality of the hostility between the two, nothing moving upon it ... Halting at a high point she stared out over the grim no-man's-land of gutted or flattened buildings that marked the battlegrounds of '75 and '76, the memories of both protagonists not permitting any rebuilding yet ...

Abruptly, she averted her eyes and walked on. But the deathly chill of that desolation stayed with her, seeming to inform even the sunlight with a lethargy that subtly mocked the natural essence of sunshine ...

Then as she was strolling back towards Shams apartments, the road empty in front of her and her footfalls soft on the dusty pavement, he erupted into the quietness of the morning. No more than twenty yards ahead of her, a man running: he had come out of a narrow alley to her left, was going away from her, a big bulky figure in a dark suit and his gait suggesting panic, a quick glance over the shoulder and then his head down again and all the time his feet pounding on –

But no-one followed. And – as standing stock-still she watched – he staggered sideways and fell to the ground. Lay sprawled face-down on the pavement, moveless.

But still no-one followed him out of the alley. She ran to him then. Crouched beside him, eased him over onto his side. Saw his face drained of colour, his mouth sagging open, eyes half-closed, only the whites showing; no detectable heart-beat, but a slightest feathering of breath between the flaccid lips. No blood to be seen anywhere about him – thank God no blood!

She got to her feet, her eyes skimming over the windows of nearby apartments, thinking to call out to someone to telephone for an ambulance, police. But all the windows remained closed (Damn them! *Someone* must have seen? Must have, yes; but no-one offers help – '*I dare not be any part of something like that when a strike's on*' – Damn them!). She began to run, up the road, and into the Shams building; hammered on the door of the ground-floor flat until Madame Nsouli opened it ...

Half an hour later, she was sitting with Tagarid, in the lounge. They were drinking whisky and water with a dash of lemon. An ambulance had answered the Nsoulis' call, its passage fast through the quiet streets; but by the time it arrived the man sprawled lumpish on the broken pavement was dead. Unhurriedly, the attendants had loaded the body into the vehicle, closed the doors upon it; and the ambulance had moved off along the road quite slowly, no need to speed now.

'You won't go back to Britain yet, will you.' Tagarid made it a statement, not a question.

Lois did not answer immediately; sat quiet, almost abstracted. Finally said: 'I won't go until after Soheil has been released, and you have made up your mind. About going to the States.'

'What happened out in the street this morning, that really got to you, didn't it?'

Drink in hand, Lois stood up and crossed to the French windows that stood open to the balcony: poinsettias and jasmine in flower out there, the lush greenery of ferns ...

'I don't think I've ever felt so lonely – so alone – as I did then,' she said slowly. 'The people in those flats, they must have *seen*; and so they must have realized what I was looking for. But – all the windows stayed closed.'

'We're afraid.'

'I wonder what – *who* he was running away from?'

'Did the ambulance men ask you about that? Didn't he have any papers?'

She shook her head. 'No papers. And they didn't want to know ... Cause of death, heart failure: once that was established, they simply wanted to be on their way.' She sipped from her glass; and then said quietly, 'Maybe he'd be alive still, if he hadn't run like that? So, desperately.'

'Maybe ... At least most of us here in Lebanon have stopped *running away* now. The hope that if you go far enough, fast enough – as some did, to other countries, leaving the majority to stay and do so mentally, intellectually – then somehow you'll be safe: that's what we believed at first, many of us. It didn't work out like that, though; and it has taken us fifteen years to accept it.'

'You yourself? You've stopped running, now?'

Tagarid gave a small laugh. 'I'm – standing still, I think. And Lebanon the same, perhaps. Standing still while we take stock and gather our strength together. Providing we're allowed time to do that.'

'But – in that physical sense you just spoke of – you'll be running away if you go to the States.'

'I'm becoming less sure all the time, about going ...' There was a silence; and then she asked, her voice deliberately casual, 'Lois. You wouldn't consider staying on here for good? If I stayed, I mean?'

Startled: 'What on earth gave you that idea?'

'Well, you were saying a day or two ago that Dan, Dan
Ferguson – that he hadn't, to put it mildly, been greatly in
your mind since you came out here … And, this Fahal
Rizik you've been seeing? I have the feeling you like him
a lot. You might – marry him?'

Slowly, head down, Lois walked back to her chair and
sat down. Drank from her glass and then put it on the
table beside her. And gave no answer because she did not
have one – neither yea nor nay – that she herself was
ready to accept. Instead:

'You think that's the reason I'm staying on now?' she
asked coldly.

'Not consciously, maybe.' Tagarid met her stare, held
it.

And after a moment Lois smiled at her sister. 'Soheil,
first,' she said. 'Now AKAL have got Mansoor
something's bound to happen. The FFP cannot stand by
and see him held captive. They'll have to deal; and God
willing, Soheil will be part of that deal.'

Arriving at Geraldine's party that evening, Lois found it
a more formal affair than she had expected: a score or so
guests, and servants handing round drinks and short
eats. Geraldine provided her with a gin and tonic, then
took her to meet Nizar, who was standing near the door
talking with another man, a small fair man who moved
away as they approached.

A surprise to her, Nizar. Older than she had imagined
– surely around forty-five – he was broad-shouldered,
physically commanding, and an air of authority about
him; as the introductions were made his light brown eyes
smiling to her, welcoming – but inquisitive also. Olive
complexion, straight greying hair; an attractive man, and

aware of it.

'You and I have a mutual acquaintance, you know,' he said as Geraldine left them together. His English was good, but a heavy accent to it.

'Really? Who's that?'

'Fahal Rizik. He's here tonight.'

In momentary confusion she looked round, asking, 'Is he? I didn't see –'

'Fahal and I have known each other for two or three years. There is a family at Baalbek, friends of both Fahal and myself –' He broke off and smiled at her. 'Please, may we speak Arabic?' he asked. 'Geraldine says you are fluent and for me it will be so much easier.'

Lois felt sure he knew she was longing to see Fahal. This annoyed her, made her *not* want to see him, or at least to cause it so to appear.

'Of course – and let's sit down,' she said, leading the way towards three easy-chairs grouped near an arrangement of indoor plants. 'Has this family lived in Baalbek long?' she asked as they sat down.

'Many generations.' He looked down at his glass. 'They are actually distant relatives of mine. My grandmother on my father's side was a Baalbekki girl.'

She had nothing but loathing and contempt for the part the Syrian government had played in the long slow disintegration of the Lebanon.

'So you came back with an army,' she said; but turned the edge of it, her voice light and conversational.

At once his mouth tightened, his eyes flashed up to hers (and she saw them for a moment hard and very bright, examining her). Then he leaned forward and set his glass down on the low table between them. When he looked at her again his face was smooth, his gaze reflective.

'Hasn't this part of the world been like that for millennia?' He put it to her quietly. 'The rich land of the Fertile Crescent; and command of the ports on the Mediterranean seaboard: those twin golden eggs the lure. The flow and counter-flow of conquerors – and would-be conquerors! – simply man's natural response to that lure.'

She was tempted to reply that she knew her history well enough, and that his 'apologia' was too simplistic anyway. Instead:

'How did you and Fahal get to be friends?' It seemed to come out of its own accord. Spoken, seemed possibly a little rude, but she stood by it, regarding him levelly, awaiting his reply – already suspecting that this was a man who could lie most convincingly were that to serve his purpose; and, that he would in all cases be very sure of what his purpose was.

'He was visiting Baalbek.' He moved his hands, almost as if to "placate" her. 'The whole thing was quite a coincidence, I suppose. You see, I like walking in the country.' He glanced at her and grinned (yes, truly a grin, a schoolboy grin, and I'd never have guessed he had it in him, Lois thought). 'That's not the prerogative of the Brits, you know,' he said. 'This day we first met, I'd taken a car across the Valley to the Nahr al Aasi – the Orontes – then set off on foot. Along the river bank ...'

'And – Fahal?'

'He was fishing. I came up behind him and he pulled a gun on me, but I wasn't carrying one so no harm got done ... We ended up fishing together. Caught six good trout and halved the catch ...'

Innocuous; amusing; entirely believable and no reason not to believe. She found herself wanting to believe. But, *did not*. Laughed with Nizar and went on talking with him and he was good company, but all the while knew herself wary of him, the friendship between this man and Fahal somehow suspect; it aroused in her a mistrust the more worrying because of its uncertainty, its lack of any solid pin-pointable foundation –

'Lois. Good evening.' Fahal spoke from behind her and she turned and greeted him. 'Come and meet a couple I know, Ilsa and Ahmed,' he suggested then; and she went with him, Nizar getting to his feet too but not accompanying them, instead turning away saying he would look for Geraldine.

Ilsa: a tall and elegant blonde, thirtyish, who taught philosophy at the Lebanese University; set off by dramatic make-up, her blue eyes were large and luminous and had that quality of secret dreaming that speaks of drugs used – so far – judiciously. At her side her Kuwaiti man-friend, educated in Switzerland and now employed at his nation's Embassy; he was shorter than Ilsa and his face was round and plump, but his wit and intelligence made the conversation highly enjoyable ... Later, other names and faces: all pleasant and courteous, some more immediately interesting than others ... A party, any place, any time ...

Lois had no further talk with Nizar that evening; but he stayed in her mind, clearly remembered, and still that tenuous sense of apprehension in her as she thought about him; unfounded, yes, *but there inside her nevertheless* ...

'Do you think Geraldine and Nizar will get married?' She put it bluntly to Fahal as he drove her home (the same borrowed Honda, she noticed).

'I hope they will.' His answer immediate, his voice warm, eager. 'I know Nizar wants it. He has taken her to visit his family, and says they approve.'

'But – an army wife? I can't see Geraldine –'

'Oh, Nizar has other plans. He intends to quit the army in a few years' time; then, he'll open a luxury hotel in Baalbek. Now the Syrians are in the Beka'a, all is quiet up there. Tourists will come as they did in the past –'

'Through Beirut? Surely not –'

'Not Beirut. Through Damascus. There is a great future in tourism to Baalbek, and Nizar has the contacts which will make it possible ...'

Fahal went on enthusiastically, detailing to her the plans of his friend Nizar. With the Syrian army keeping the peace throughout eastern Lebanon, Baalbek would come to life again: safe passage to its archaeological glories and peaceful enjoyment of them being once more guaranteed, tourists would flood in as they had before 'the Troubles', and their money would revitalize the town –

'Pax Romana, Syrian style,' she said. Thinking: and Lebanon robbed, Syria will take for herself all that is worth taking.

He glanced at her sharply; and drove on in silence. We're close to home anyway, she thought, and what does any of it matter to him, he's Palestinian not Lebanese. And me? I've no right to hand out criticism – because I've kept myself clear of it, haven't I? ... *Haven't I?*'

A few minutes later Fahal pulled up outside the Shams building, choosing a place directly beneath one of the four street-lamps spaced along the kerb there, marking out and claiming the area reserved for (and maintained by) its residents. Coming round to her side of the car, he opened the door for her to get out; and as she did so, took both her hands in his.

'*Take care*,' he said.

She saw his face tense in the light of the lamp, as though he sought to convey to her by his words a lot more than their usual casual message of farewell. And suddenly he seemed to her very young and somehow – unsure? Disturbed, she smiled tentatively.

'I always do that,' she said. But left her hands in his.

'No, please, I'm serious.'

She looked into his eyes closely then; and found no youthful vulnerability in them.

'What do you mean?' she asked him.

He let go of her hands, stepped back (and the light of the lamp, angled differently now, shadowed his face to that of a stranger).

'The city is a dangerous place,' he said.

'For a woman alone?'

'Yes, that.' He seized upon it – embroidered upon it swiftly, going on. 'You walk around by yourself too much, Lois. To and from the Academy – and then this morning, it was foolish to go out like that when a strike had been ordered ... I, I worry about you; knowing the things you do.'

Across a silence, they felt each other out, each keeping within the parameters of their own desired secrecy. After a moment:

'Thank you,' she said softly. 'I thank you for that.' And then she let that lie in its own place, deliberately moved away from it, asking him, 'How's it going, your application for the Saudi visa?'

'It progresses ... I'm not in such a hurry as I was, now.'

'Why?'

'I think you know why.' He stepped close to her again (his face open to the light once more, and she knew he meant it to be that way, open to *her*). 'I *hope* you know?' he said.

She nodded. 'I know. And I'm glad.'

'Stay here in Beirut for a while, Lois.'

'I've made no plans to return to Britain.'

'Because of your sister? And Soheil Fanous?'

'That's – part of it. Yes, of course. I shan't leave her until this is over and he's a free man. There are other things, though.' Then she smiled; and "played back" to him his own prevarications of a few moments before, saying, 'I think you know what those other things are. I *hope* you know?'

… As a minute later she walked away from him across the courtyard she asked herself why it was that each of them seemed to need to hold back from stating to the other, without ambivalence: I love you.

Then, surveyed her own suggested answer thoughtfully: it is because we are playing for time. Each of us, for our private reasons, *playing for time* …

Well I know why I am doing that. *But why is Fahal …?*

Eleven

The day a strike is in progress: a good time to travel the city, to hold a meeting to hammer out the logistics of an operation already agreed on in principle by two opposed militias. Provided of course that the men behind the guns holding the streets obediently quiet know the number, make, colour of your car. Which in this case they certainly do …

Abu Hamad in personal negotiation with Saleh Badr: high-level FFP talking face-to-face with his equivalent within the AKAL hierarchy. A singular occurrence, between such bitter enemies. But present circumstances had forced each Group to acknowledge a need for discussions to take place between empowered representatives: an exchange of hostages may be agreed in principle with relative ease, but the implementation of such an exchange requires the most stringent safeguards since past history advises – *dictates* – a total and mutual distrust between the two engaged parties.

Each man had brought with him an aide-de-camp, an administrative officer to take notes of the procedures finally agreed upon. The 'broker' in the exchange had been secured previously: a prominent member of the national business fraternity, he had accepted his dangerous role because he perceived the situation to be nearing explosion point; if Mansoor were not soon a free man there would be bloody battle in the streets of Beirut. And it wouldn't stop there – it never had before …

'Mansoor to be delivered by us to the broker's residence, under guard, between 10 and 11 o'clock on the morning of the 22nd May.' Badr summed up their discussion on this point, the starting-point, eyeing Abu Hamad coldly. He wished him dead. Furiously resented having to meet him, having to sit across a table and talk man-to-man with this, this enemy, this detested individual who never in the whole of life could ever possibly be anything else but, *enemy*.

'Once Mansoor is in his hands, the broker will telephone headquarters FFP.' Abu Hamad watching his opponent's eyes. (And his aide, observant of the two protagonists, thought: they would both prefer to fight it out in blood; but that, neither side dares risk at the moment, Big Brother Syria would set his own men on them if they tried that and the Groups small-fry then.) 'I myself will await the call. Once certain that he is safely placed with the broker, I will give orders for the next move in the operation, the freeing of our hostages, to commence.'

Discussion proceeded. Every move in the forthcoming exchange was gone into in depth. Each detail of each separate arrangement put forward was examined exhaustively and suspiciously for hidden pitfalls, until finally agreement had been reached on every step necessary to bring the exercise to a successful conclusion. Then, after a last run-through, allowing each side to make quite certain that no possible advantage to the other had been allowed to slip in unnoticed, the meeting broke up. No handshakes; merely a mutual turning of the back …

Abu Hamad was driven away by Ramadan Saad, travelling through the city towards Rue 22, to the basement stronghold of FFP. There, he ordered Saad to accompany him; and made his way to the smaller of the two conference rooms. Three men were awaiting him, seated in upright chairs at the table: FFP area commanders, each of them in charge of one of the small groups of AKAL men seized hostage on 8th May. Indicating a place for Saad at the far end of the table, Abu Hamad sat down with his commanders and proceeded to brief them on the events now scheduled to take place in two days' time.

Thus: each group of prisoners (two or three men, as the case might be) was to be conducted to a certain (specified) place. That done, one of two methods for the return of each man to his own home was to be employed: either a relative was to be contacted and given the information necessary to collect him, or he was simply to be left to make his own way – choice between the two procedures at each commander's discretion. On two further matters, however, there was no choice: each released AKAL man was required to get to his home with all possible speed; and once arrived there, was immediately to telephone a certain number (supplied) and report himself free and unharmed. It was each commander's duty to impress upon the men he was releasing that compliance with these two obligations was essential; were either one neglected, the other comrades' safety would very quickly be at risk ...

As Abu Hamad was speaking, the three commanders made notes from time to time; and then when he invited their questions, asked for clarification on a few details. Minor queries only, until:

'Sir.' The youngest man present: wirily built and

hawk-faced; and determined to make his mark with his leader who had been his idol since boyhood. 'The agreement on the exchange, made between ourselves and AKAL. If all goes according to plan, does it guarantee future immunity from attack for all the hostages concerned?'

Abu Hamad glanced at him keenly. 'An interesting point,' he observed (and the questioner perceived himself noted with approval). 'Outside the scope of this briefing, but undoubtedly interesting ... The answer is: yes. The FFP and AKAL have each guaranteed all hostages involved in this exchange immunity from further attack – provided they do not engage in active operations – for a period of six months ... Further questions?' As he looked into their faces he found there the hard self-confidence he had expected. And when each had indicated himself satisfied, proceeded to the final item on his agenda.

'One last thing, then,' he said. 'Each of you now to read out to me the names of the hostages you hold.'

They did as ordered. Abu Hamad sat listening. So did Ramadan Saad; and when the last commander fell silent, Saad realized that he had heard only seven names. Did a mental check, and concluded that *the name of Soheil Fanous had not been spoken* ...

The commanders were dismissed. But Abu Hamad made no move to leave; sat hunched in his chair, head down; and silent. At last straightened, looked across at Saad.

'Go along to the office,' he ordered. 'There's a man I called in, Fanous' interrogator. Get him in here ... And bring me coffee. Turkish.'

Saad found the interrogator waiting, sitting in one of the visitors' chairs, leafing through a magazine, an air of

controlled impatience to him. The Turkish took longer:
for Abu Hamad it must be freshly made ...

His coffee in front of him, the FFP leader surveyed
the man he had summoned: he was familiar with his
work, and had confidence in his perceptions – in his
preferred methods, also, although those had caused
adverse comment in some quarters in the past.
However, he reflected, that side of 'interrogation' had
not featured in the case of the man he was about to
discuss. (Saad also was studying – but more covertly –
the man he had escorted in. Until this day he had
known him by repute only: and now found his cool
self-assurance before Abu Hamad impressive, backed as
it was by the inquisitive intelligence distinguishing the
grey eyes, by the cruelty lined into the thin-lipped
mouth ...)

'The hostage Soheil Fanous.' Abu Hamad flung the
name down on the table between them like the mailed
glove of challenge. (That slaying of his daughter has
brought all the viciousness in him boiling to the surface
again, thought Saad. He's insatiable now as he was in the
old days; he'd like to see every member of AKAL dead
in their own blood, would gladly undertake each and
every killing himself if he thought he could get away
with it.) 'What were your final conclusions about him?'

'In what particular respect?' Privately, the
interrogator considered Abu Hamad a "thug", one of
that old school of mindless violence whose practitioners
still – in his opinion, voiced occasionally in secret to
others of like mind – held far too much power in the
turmoil that was national politics, using it as they did to
bludgeon into second place the counsel of those who
favoured a more cerebral and devious approach to their
enemies. However, for all his own ruthlessness, he also

feared him; and had resolved to give him full co-operation in this case, which was of considerable importance to the two Groups involved and might yet assist his own advancement in some way, if he handled things well.

'Two. First: is he telling the truth when he claims that he is not a fully participating member of AKAL?'

The interrogator had no need to think over his reply: expecting some such question, he had prepared a considered answer.

'I was able to form no definite, incontrovertible opinion on that point,' he said. 'Clearly Fanous has had contact with AKAL, for on his own admission he has helped members of that Group; but, it seems, in ways that were purely professional. Matters of personal health and welfare.'

'No more than that? You were unable to shake him?' The voice edged.

'He told his story and held to it under questioning. I tried drugs, but to no avail. He conducted himself cleverly throughout interrogation.'

'Come on, man! Don't play about. Commit yourself one way or the other. I need a straight answer.'

'If I must give you one ... It is my opinion that Fanous may be more important within the AKAL Group-structure than he admits.'

Abu Hamad leaned forward across the desk, his eyes narrowed. 'So now to the second question,' he said. 'Given what you have just said, and in the light of all you have learned from him – and about him – during your interrogations, do you think Fanous knows, or holds a position within AKAL which would enable him to find out, the identity of the man who ordered the attack on my car during which my daughter was killed?'

The interrogator always took care to keep himself well informed regarding men and affairs likely to affect his own position: he knew of Abu Hamad's desire for revenge, and was not prepared to allow himself to be isolated as the man who had stood in the way of it.

'I think *it is possible* he knows, or is in a position to be able to discover the identity of the man you want.'

'That's all?' The voice jabbing at him. 'You, who had the interrogation of him, let him get away with –'

'*I repeat, it is possible –*'

'Interrogators come up with facts, not possibilities. You're a fool. A dangerous incompetent!'

The interrogator got to his feet, stood to attention. 'With respect, you are being offensive. I had no powers. My instructions forbade physical coercion.'

'Leave!' But even as the man turned away: 'Wait!' Abu Hamad ordered. And then stood up and stared the interrogator in the eyes. ' "It is possible". Your words. You stand by them?'

'Sir!' A formal military acquiescence.

'Would your knowledge of Fanous allow you to advance that to "*probable*"?'

The interrogator took his time to answer. He was aware that his future career – perhaps even his life – lay in the balance here: those inferiors who refused to go in the direction Abu Hamad indicated as his own preference invariably found their future promotion blocked, and there had been one at least who had fallen victim to an 'accident' later tainted by certain peculiar circumstances surrounding it.

At last:

'Probable,' he conceded thoughtfully. Gave a small nod of finality. 'Yes, in the light of all my dealings with Fanous: *probable*.'

Abu Hamad waved a dismissal, then sat down facing his long-time comrade Ramadan Saad.

'A fool indeed,' he observed. 'But an ambitious one, and how useful that combination can be … You marked what he said? "*Probable*"?'

'I marked it.'

'Remember it. Questions could be asked, later.'

Looking into his face, Saad saw his eyes – predatory. 'Fanous – his name didn't show on your field-commanders' lists,' he said quietly, for it seemed to him important that he should understand what he was committing himself to in working so closely with his leader.

'He is to be dealt with separately from the others. I arranged it, earlier.'

'Your purpose, in so doing?' Daring it, because of the special relationship between them.

'I have selected him as the instrument of my revenge … One way or another.'

'You mean, you will try to get from him the name of the man you seek? But his interrogator –'

'The interrogator was forbidden to use the methods we all know to be most likely to produce results. I am not fettered in a like manner.'

'Torture?'

A thin smile. 'Of a certain kind.'

'But – where? In God's name, how? He has to be freed, it's agreed with AKAL. In two days' time he'll be a free man, in his own home.'

'That is where we shall, pressure him.' The smile had reached Abu Hamad's eyes now. 'His own home: probably the one place where a man like Fanous may successfully be exposed to certain choices he has not expected and therefore has not equipped himself to deal with.'

Saad looked down. Priorities had to be established and then acted upon. Immediately. Economically, in the silence of his mind, he examined and evaluated his loyalties. There was the Group, of which both he himself and Abu Hamad were, in their widely differing capacities, active members; and meshed within that tightly-structured tissue was the integer named Ramadan Saad-Abu Hamad. The Group had put its mark to a bargain with an enemy; in pursuance of his own personal aims and desires Abu Hamad planned to rupture the terms of that bargain within, it seemed, hours of its fulfilment. *Where do I stand in this conflict of commitment?*

The self-examination produced decision swiftly since there was in truth no argument once the challengers for his loyalty had stood forward and declared themselves: Saad accepted in full the implications of Abu Hamad's words "That is where we shall pressure him". *We.*

'You plan to move against him, when?' he asked, looking up.

'The day of the exchange. Provided of course that no last-minute development advises postponement. We'll get at him while he's still high on the fact he's escaped.' It had not occurred to Abu Hamad to *request* the assistance of his old friend; he had simply *assumed* that loyalty to be available to him, immediate and unquestioning and if necessary to the death: assumed, *because that was what he would accord to Ramadan Saad were it ever to be required of him.*

'We work alone? Just you and I?' For "official" FFP would be certain to seek to distance themselves from any such action lest it stain their "honour" in the eyes of the citizens – be seen as an outrage violating their given word.

'Inside the Fanous apartment, only you and I.'

'But you'll have men outside?'

'Two or three. Just in case. They won't be briefed in advance on what's going to happen inside. Obviously they'll know later, but they will not be told what is to be done by we two. Only three people will know that: us; and Fahal Rizik.'

'How does he enter into it?'

'He knows the layout of the apartment. Also, he has contact with the other woman, the wife's sister.' He stood up and led the way towards the door. 'I want to know as much as possible about all those who will be in that apartment when we move in. Tagarid Fanous; Lois Everard; Liliane Ansari. Rizik can tell us about them. I will explain to him how I expect to develop the situation, and see how he thinks each will react to what is taking place. That could be important ... Contact Rizik, arrange a meeting between the three of us. Make it for tomorrow morning. Ten o'clock ...'

The next evening, as had become their custom after the 6 to 8 class, Lois and Fahal went together to the café 'Sesame'.

'You were inattentive today,' she mock-reprimanded him as, returning to their table from the service counter, he placed her coffee in front of her and then sat down opposite. (Never beside her, she had noticed that; and told herself it was because he enjoyed having her face fully open to his eyes; but suspected in her heart that it was the Arab in him laying it down as unseemly for a man to be seen in a public place seated too close to a girl who was not his near relative ... I must ask him about it, she had told herself; but she had not yet done so. Perhaps I will tonight, now, she thought. But then looking up into his eyes found them – keeping her at a distance? Maybe. Or maybe he's simply tired …?)

She had spoken in English. He answered in the same language.

'I am sorry you found me such a poor student,' he said. Put a smile on his face then, and added carefully, 'Please, not "inattentive". The word must be "abstracted", I think. Or should it be "dis-tracted"?'

'That depends on –' But she broke off, seeing his feeble attempt at a smile already failed; and his eyes meeting hers but setting up barriers against them. 'What's wrong?' she asked.

He picked up his cup and drank half his coffee. 'This place is crummy,' he said, speaking in Arabic now, leaning his elbows on the table and looking around him with distaste.

'Cheap, yes; but not crummy. The tables are too close together and there's no wall-to-wall carpeting and your sugar is rationed to two little paper packets per person, no bowl to help yourself from. But it's clean; and the people who come here, they're ordinary and just fine. No weirdos.'

'And no muzak.' He sat back, relaxing. 'Thank God, no muzak. We can talk to each other.'

But the effort it had cost him was too apparent. 'What's the matter?' she asked again.

'Nothing.' I cannot handle this, he was saying to himself. Just can't handle it. That meeting this morning, Abu Hamad milking me of information about her, and about the interior layout of the apartment. Then referring to me throughout, to check the suitability of each move they'll make once they're inside the flat, as he and Ramadan Saad worked out step by step the mechanics of the hit they plan to make against Soheil Fanous –

'Is there still difficulty about the Saudi visa?' She searched his face but he would not meet her eyes.

He seized on this with relief. 'They called me in again this morning. Some fiddling little hurdle yet to be negotiated, apparently. But I'm afraid it's deliberate. They'll demand – more.' Haven't I earned it even yet? ... And *she will be in there*. When Abu Hamad and Saad go in, she'll be there inside. 'You got the keys?' Abu Hamad asked. 'Surely,' Saad answered. 'Paid the servant the sum agreed on, and guaranteed that the action threatened against her son in Damascus will be called off' –

'More money? Is that it?' Lois put it to him angrily, conscious that he was in some way evading her, half his mind elsewhere.

'What else?' In sudden panic: if she learns anything of the truth before Abu Hamad moves against Fanous, and therefore they find themselves *expected* when they go into that apartment – I am a dead man, then. They, Abu Hamad and Saad – or others, if they themselves are killed – will mark me as the only one who could have betrayed them; and from that moment *I am a dead man* ...

'I'll put up what you need. You know that.' She had glimpsed the sudden naked fear in him; and it was in her to give him more money if that was all that was required. I'm not poor and he is: he's young and the money will buy him into a new life in a country at peace with itself (relative to Lebanon, anyway) ... Yes I would like to give him that.

At her words, Fahal's face quietened. Tension

drained out of him and he sat forward, towards her. For a few seconds he said nothing, simply looked at her (and it seemed to her that all 'outside' things had fallen away from him, there was at that moment only himself and her in his mind).

But then he drew back; and all he said was: 'You're very generous. Thank you for offering to help again.'

'I'll need a couple of days, to get it from the bank. Otherwise, no problem.' Deliberately offhand; and she drained her coffee and stood up. 'Let's go. I'll take a taxi, from Rashid's.' Rashid Salim's two sons were studying at Leila's, and his garage had been used by many of the students over the years; his taxi service was long established as reliable and had a clean bill of "safety" of both the physical and political kind.

So Lois arrived at the Shams building; let herself into the apartment with her key. As she entered the lounge, Tagarid came in through the French windows giving access to the balcony. She had been tending the pot-plants and had a small long-tined fork in her hand.

'Soheil's going to be freed,' she said, casually almost.

'*When*?' Lois dropped her holdall to the floor, ran to her sister.

'Tomorrow. Details later; apparently it's part of some complicated deal –'

'How did you get the news?'

'The AKAL man who came here before, he rang up about an hour ago and told me.' She made a small grimace of distaste. 'I recognized his voice,' she said; and wrapping her gardening fork in plastic put it down on a table, beside a vase of flowers. 'A peculiar grating quality it had … God, my hands are filthy. I'll go and clean up.' She began to move towards the door.

'Tagarid!' Her sister turned, and Lois saw the

beautiful face tense and hard, drawn in upon itself.
'Don't just – walk away! *Tell me!*'

'Nothing to tell, yet. Except what I said before, he'll be
released tomorrow.' She frowned; and tried to make
words for the feelings inside her. 'You set the sights of
the whole of your existence on one particular thing,' she
said, 'waiting for that, willing it to be, or happen. Then
it does, and suddenly you're not sure any more ... Not
sure in regard to anything that's to do with that
particular "priority desire" of yours which dominated
your life for so long.' She shook her head, staring at the
flowers in the vase beside her gardening fork; reached
out a hand and withdrew a rose, re-positioned it in the
floral arrangement; and then, finally, voiced the bleak
fact secreted at the centre of her anguish. 'It terrifies
me!' she said.

'What does, exactly?'

Tagarid looked at her then; and after a moment gave
a small hard laugh.

'You: yes, *you* I can tell,' she said. 'I'm terrified
because whatever happens now between Soheil and me,
it will never again be the same as it was, before, between us.
And that overwhelms me. I don't know. Loneliness, I
suppose. A whole section of my life exposed as having
been based on one totally false premise. It's a sort of
loneliness.'

'But – when you phoned me in the UK – by then you
must already have thought things through. *You* planned
to leave *him*, not the other way round.'

'All true. I know I'm not being logical. But people
aren't always, are they?' She essayed a smile; and then,
carefully, stepped clear of what had been said between
them. Her face softened a little. 'He didn't say much,
the AKAL man,' she went on, voice and manner

returned to poised assurance. 'Told me the FFP have agreed an exchange because they've got to get Mansoor back. Other hostages besides Soheil are to be freed by FFP, and on release each of them has to comply with a certain set of instructions. Neither side trusts the other, of course, so the safeguards against double-dealing are mandatory – he said if we don't abide by them, in each and every detail, the exchange won't go through.'

'So – what happens tomorrow? What do we do?'

'We have to pick Soheil up somewhere, the FFP won't bring him into the city. And they won't reveal the pick-up point until one hour before the time, either. The whole thing will be run to a very tight schedule, apparently. We get a phone call around noon, telling us where he'll be. We drive out there, at once. Only one person to go.'

Her repeated use of the word 'we': the possible implication attendant upon that pronoun suddenly dawned on Lois.

'*Who* drives out to collect him?' she asked.

'The AKAL man said that didn't matter, provided it's someone who knows Beirut and the country to the south-east of it within a radius of twenty kilometres. Also, naturally, it has to be someone Soheil will accept as *bona fide* … Will you go, Lois? I'll phone Leila, explain …'

'Why not you?'

'I'd rather meet him – here. I couldn't face it: meeting at some roadside, and then the drive back together … Will you?'

It did not seem much to give. Lois gave it, gladly. But by the end of the next day was to wonder what the outcome would have been had she chosen to withhold that particular gift.

Twelve

The promised call did not come until a little before one o'clock. They had all got up at their usual times; Liliane had departed at nine-thirty; and then Lois and Tagarid (having received from their respective employers leave-of-absence for the day) had applied themselves to living through the hours of waiting, each in her own fashion.

How differently we even *wait*, thought Lois, watching her sister moving in her efficient self-possessed way about the various household tasks she had set herself, for she had telephoned Salaam the previous evening to tell her to take the day off, not to come in for work until Wednesday. Remembering then, Lois, that Tagarid had smiled as she put the phone down. 'Salaam seemed pleased,' she had said. 'Nice, I suppose, a whole day free, unexpectedly. She didn't even ask me *why* ...' And now this morning Tagarid has proceeded methodically through the necessary chores while I have been a damn nuisance – to her and to myself! – unable to settle to anything, making grand offers to help but then when given something to do either skimping it or leaving it altogether and going to stare out of some nearby window and think, no not even properly think, merely 'wonder if' this or that ...

Just once Tagarid's calm cracked. At 11.15 the phone rang; she picked up the receiver, turning her back on me. Listened for perhaps five seconds before gritting out 'Get off the bloody line!' and slamming the thing down. Returned to polishing silver then; but her hands were trembling. I found that outburst less puzzling than her earlier poise …

Ten minutes to one. For the second time that morning, the phone rang and Tagarid answered it. This time, listened and did not break the connection –

'Yes, this is Madame Fanous … No. No, my sister will fetch him … Lois Everard. She is here … Yes of course. Wait a moment.' She held out the receiver. 'AKAL. He wants to speak to you since you're the one going.'

Instructions, a phone number: Lois listened, and made notes on the pad beside the phone. And when finally he asked, 'Is everything clear to you? If anything is not, you may now ask questions. Otherwise I will end the call.'

She had no questions. As she put the phone down:

'What did he say?' Tagarid demanded, standing close beside her.

Lois summarized the directions she had been given. Drive twelve kilometres out of Beirut on the Aramoun road, turn off that onto the first left-hand (dirt) road beyond Al Ain. Three kilometres along that, a derelict farmhouse (stone) set back about half a kilometre from the track, not too difficult to see provided you're looking for it: within its walls, Soheil would be awaiting the pick-up. No-one else would be there.

'When?' Tagarid's voice sharp; her face impassive. 'You're to go straightaway?'

'Yes, now.' She glanced at her watch. 'We haven't got much time.'

'What's that phone number? The one you wrote
down?'

'There are three "orders" to be carried out. One, I am
to drive Soheil straight back here. Second, as soon as
he's here he's to ring that number and report himself
safely home – he'll know he has to do that, but he won't
know the number to ring. And third, Soheil is not to go
out of the apartment, nor is he or any of us to invite
anyone else *into* the apartment, until he is informed, by
AKAL, that he may do so –'

'That's when I heard you say, "Why? In God's name,
why"? What did he answer?'

'It made sense; I felt a fool for asking ... There are in
all eight AKAL hostages involved in the exchange. The
safe return of each and every one must be completed
and centrally verified before moves proceed for the
"broker" to release the FFP man, Al Jaffer Mansoor.
Time is needed for all that.'

'I'd been thinking to invite one or two of his
colleagues from the hospital in for drinks this evening –'

'You haven't done anything about it, though?'

Tagarid shook her head. 'No, not yet.' She grimaced,
and turned away. 'I won't believe it, until he's actually
here. And I won't ask anyone now, obviously. So we'll
have the whole evening alone, Soheil and I, you, and
Liliane ...'

The men's rooming-house where Fahal Rizik lived was a
cheap place, purpose-built and strictly functional.
Ramadan Saad had himself inhabited many such in his
time and made his way up the unswept concrete
stairway to the third floor entirely unworried by the
litter underfoot, the graffiti inscribed on the
whitewashed walls.

He studied the look of surprise on Rizik's face when he opened the door to him – perceived no guilt in it and was glad of that, for the boy showed promise and the intelligent ones like him were not so easily recruited these days, too many of them wanted only one thing and that was to get out of Lebanon ...

The room he stepped into was sparsely furnished, but clean. Student posters on the walls, worn mats on the floor, a small curtained-off recess, its half-open curtains revealing a rudimentary kitchen. He seated himself in a cushioned armchair, waved Rizik to sit down again in the chair at the desk, books and papers strewn about on it, obviously he'd been working on something.

Rizik remained standing. 'Would you like coffee, a cool drink?' he asked. 'It won't take long –'

'Nothing. This is not a social call.'

Rizik grinned. 'I didn't think it was,' he said. He drew an upright chair close in front of his visitor then, and sat down facing him. 'Something's come up?' he asked soberly.

Saad took his time to answer, sitting relaxed, silent, his eyes taking further stock of the room before finally returning to the boy's face and studying that. Strange how in my mind I always perceive him as 'boy', he thought, when in fact he can only be fourteen or fifteen years younger than me. But then those extra years that make me the older one – they were lived during a period of our civil war that was particularly vicious, even for us. A war often carried on underground, yes; but then possibly that's a situation which circumscribes and in the end stunts the mind? Having no contact at all – on the *thinking* level – with the other side, your mind ceases to question outwards, finally ceases to question at all: you simply label the whole lot of them 'enemy' and then let the emotions take over, dictate the inevitable response ...

'The exchange of hostages will be implemented today,' he said finally. And watching, saw Rizik's eyes narrow, saw a guarded look come into them. Knew then that he had been right to come: as a precaution, surely no more than that.

'You want me – in the apartment with you? You've come to brief me?'

'No. Abu Hamad sent me to ask you about Lois Everard.'

Rizik's face expressionless under the searching stare of the man whom he suddenly saw as his inquisitor. Blandly:

'I've told you all I know about her,' he said.

'Except, I think, for one particular aspect of your various dealings with her.' Abruptly, Saad sat forward, and his voice as he went on was hard, attacking – yet there was mockery in it as well. 'Ahmed came better out of your bargain than you did,' he said. 'You disobeyed a clear order, both of you.'

'How did you know?' Stupid question, he castigated himself as soon as the words were out: there was only one way they *could* know.

'To Ahmed, the radio; to Fahal, the gold chain with the scarab: a secret between friends, inviolate of course.' The mockery cutting at the ego now.

Rizik got up and turned away. 'Ahmed – he told you?'

'It troubled his conscience and he "confessed" this morning ... The radio, yes, we understand that, Abu Hamad and I. An uncomplicated flash of greed, a youthful peccadillo. But the necklace – that is another thing altogether. Tell me why you took it. *And face me!*' The last words snapped like a whip.

Rizik obeyed, a swift jerky movement, but then he held himself well.

'I am no better than Ahmed,' he said steadily. 'I coveted it. It is old work, the scarab; and exquisitely carved.'

'We have no place in our ranks for thieves. Return it.' Saad's dark face unmoving in its stern regard; but the rebuke delivered, he at once returned to the matter of greater import. 'The woman herself is nothing to you, then?' he asked.

'Nothing.' He heard his own voice, suitably unworried; and thus discovered that to lie with confidence when your life is at stake was a talent he possessed.

'You have not said anything to her of our plans to pressure Soheil Fanous this evening, after he has returned to his apartment a free man?'

'I have not.'

Saad stood up and stepped close to Rizik; held his eyes.

'You belong *to us*.' Harshly, he laid it on the line. 'There must be no other – *love* – in your life and the living of it. A wife, yes; children, yes, in time. But *love*: you will reserve that – in all its facets – for us.'

'I know it.' At that moment, Lois Everard had no place in any part of him: he did indeed "belong" to Ramadan Saad and all he stood for.

'You have only one viable future *and it lies with the FFP*.' Saad watched the "boy" absorb it; and then released his eyes. 'You will not leave this house again until tomorrow morning,' he instructed, moving away towards the door. 'A man will be posted.'

'You do not trust me?'

Saad turned, regarded him in silence for a moment. Then:

'You made a mistake, taking the pendant,' he said. 'A

stupid mistake, no more than that; and young men do make stupid mistakes, it should not be allowed to blight their future careers provided they have talent ... I believe you to be loyal. But Abu Hamad and I will be playing for high stakes tonight. And apart from us two, you alone are aware of what we intend to do once we're inside that apartment ... Yes, I trust you, Fahal Rizik. But when my life is at risk, I believe in taking all possible precautions against all possible eventualities.' He smiled grimly. 'Once, in similar circumstances, many years ago, my judgment was at fault.' He looked down, stood silent.

Staring at him, Rizik sensed in him a guilt, a private mourning; and kept very still, feeling the two of them close as they had never been before. Comradeship: the word formed itself in his mind and he looked at it and understood.

Abruptly, Saad turned away.

'The violent deaths of friends are not easily forgotten,' he said. And went out then.

Fahal locked the door upon his going. And thus alone, found Lois Everard walking about inside his head again. *Again.*

She drove out of the city in Tagarid's car, a silver-grey Peugeot. The streets weren't as busy as earlier or later in the day and she made good time through the dreary eastern suburbs. It was only as she left the tenement blocks behind her and pulled clear of the straggling roadside garages and transport cafés that it really came home to her: in half an hour from now I shall see Soheil and he'll be a free man!

At the proper realization of this fact, a sense of exhilaration surged through her and she put her foot down and took the car speeding up the climb into the foothills. The afternoon was warm, the sun shining out of a cloudless sky ... But then she came to Sohar. Town fought through twice in '76, pounded by the unremitting shellfire of winners who then became losers only to win again three days later: the once-beautiful main street was colonnaded with ruined houses now, gaunt spectres of a murdered prosperity ... It was soon left behind; but the brightness of the sunshine had been stripped of its special element of joy.

She drove on ... No need to hurry, anyway. The instructions stipulated 'Not before two o'clock' and I must follow them to the letter ... Obedience to the 'writ' of the Groups the way of life for ordinary citizens ... 'They who live by obedience shall die by obedience'? For in obeying the dictates of one lot, you may only too easily fall foul of one of the opposing lots. Also, there are other kinds of death, aren't there?

What if Soheil isn't there? Or if this whole thing is some sort of trap? For it seems you can never be sure, in this country now, that anything or any set-up – or any*one* come to that – is on the level, is to be trusted. A creeping paralysis of honour, *of plain simple goodwill between men*: like a disease, it is consuming – or has already consumed? Dreadful thought, dig a hole for it, dig deep and cover it quick – the living flesh of Lebanon ...

'For God's sake!' She muttered the words aloud, straightening up behind the wheel, giving her head a quick shake and blinking her eyes. And the world fell back into place again. Up to a point ...

She looked at her watch: 1.35; and according to the mileage gauge she'd already travelled twelve-thirteen kilometres. Soon now she would come to Al Ain, the place referred to by her 'instructor' on the phone. She knew it well enough, it was a landmark on the highway through the foothills, a sprawling farming village set among market-gardens. As she passed through it she saw women and children working in the fields; and just beyond it had to pull onto the grassed verge to allow passage to a small convoy of army vehicles, all Syrian, a flag-flying limousine bracketed by two cars, and six attendant motor-cyclists.

Driving on, she came to a dirt road branching off to her left and as earlier directed turned onto it. It led quite steeply up towards an outcrop of grey rock; passing close beside that, dropped down again into a sheer-sided valley. Rough going now, the potholed track winding its way between tumbled boulders. Ahead of her, the valley narrowed, looked to be almost walled-in by tall rock-faces. Glancing at her watch she saw it was ten minutes to two; and stopped the car, for there could only be a kilometre or so left to go and the order had been strict, 'Not before two'. After a moment, assailed by a sudden sense of being cooped up, imprisoned almost, she got out and stood by the open door looking around her. The quietness seemed absolute; the valley, lifeless. And peculiarly hostile: its air stale and dusty, its craggy enclosing slopes forbidding – forbidding what? Nothing specific ... Don't be fanciful, it is merely a valley. Lonely and sterile, refusing succour to life of any kind ...

Getting back into the car, she drove on. And reaching the end of the valley found that the track turned sharply right, ran along between two walls of rock and then dropped down once more. But this time into a narrow fertile plain: clearly there must be a watercourse of some kind, underground maybe, for coarse grass grew everywhere, and shade-giving trees. The greenness ˌa beneficence to the eyes; and then when she rolled down the side window the smell of green things growing coming into the car.

The gauge showed she had travelled four kilometres from the highway. Searching the terrain ahead, she could see no sign of a building: but a little further on, to her right, there was an area where the trees massed together more closely, seemed to swarm up over the summit of a small rise …?

It was there, as 'he' had told her it would be: a derelict farmhouse set back a few hundred metres from the track she was on, roofless, its walls of grey stone. Being among trees as it was – again as 'he' had said – you could easily fail to see it unless you knew where to look.

She drove on a little way; then stopped the car, and got out. Started walking towards the ruin: uphill, the leaves of the trees around her whispering in a light breeze and sandy soil underfoot. She had imagined Soheil running out to meet her, for he would hear the car; but perceived no sound or movement other than her own. And coming out from under the trees found herself at the edge of an open space that had once been cobbled but the stones now mostly overgrown with moss and a yellow-flowering weed. Facing her and no more than twenty paces away was the doorless entrance to the ruin, shadows and sunlight seen on the broken floor within.

Crossing the courtyard she went in through the doorway. And found Soheil in there. He was standing in the shadowed part of the square 'room'. Was as remembered: tall wiry strength of him vital with latent energy; eyes – yes, as always his eyes compel your immediate attention, their brilliance reaching out to you, seeking your trust and giving his to you freely.

'You're alone?' he demanded, making no move towards her.

She controlled the emotion welling up inside her. Said: 'There's no-one with me.'

'No-one else, out there in the car?'

'I was instructed to come alone, so I did … You're all right?'

He stepped forward then, crossed from shadow into sunlight and stood in front of her. 'Lois.' He spoke her name quietly, studying her face (and holding his eyes, she sensed him moving back into a world entirely different from the one he had recently been inhabiting – but doing that slowly and with intense suspicion). He rapped out, 'What other instructions were you given?'

Briefly, she detailed them. Saw him listening, frowning down at the ground at his feet. He looked tired, pale, his hair needed cutting, and his clothes – a shirt and jeans – were not his own. Finally:

'You seem very mistrustful about your release,' she said.

He looked up at her then.

'I am,' he answered, grim-faced. But abruptly his mood changed – as if suddenly he'd accepted the reality of his freedom, Lois thought. He smiled and moved towards her. 'God, let's get out of this,' he said, putting an arm round her shoulders and urging her towards the door. 'How long will it take us to get home from here? Wherever "here" may be?'

'You don't know where you are?' Laughing, she went out into sunlight and led the way across the yellow-flowered courtyard.

'They blindfolded me, took me from where they were holding me – sometime mid-morning – then drove me around for a while. Finally dumped me off at this place.'

'We'll be back in forty-five minutes …'

Soheil drove. She fed him coffee, sandwiches, at the wheel. While they were on the dirt road she told him all was well at home, then asked him, carefully, what his imprisonment had been like. As he spoke of that, she sensed an exultation in him, especially when he was telling her about the times he'd been interrogated; but soon she returned their conversation to personal matters for here was an opportunity to do so with him in private.

'Soheil, why don't you and Tagarid have a child?' she asked. Sensed his immediate resentment and added, 'Please talk about it. I love her.'

After a pause he spoke, seriously, almost formally.

'There are two things in my life,' he said, not looking at her. 'The first is my work; in that I know myself extraordinarily gifted and I intend to use, develop and extend my gift. Which intention, if it is to be fulfilled, will necessitate my studying and working abroad because that is where the most up-to-date techniques are being tried and tested.'

He fell silent. She continued to watch him, and saw his profiled face expressionless. Prompted him then, asking:

'So, what is the second "thing"?' Realizing with sadness that it would not be "Tagarid".

'The Lebanon. And therefore, inevitably, our national politics; and therefore – again inevitably, given the realities of our history and present situation – the battle between the various Groups to determine which faction is to rule. A long-running battle; and it will be to the death –'

'Even if that death is Lebanon's own?'

Almost he brushed it aside, going on in his precise voice as if elucidating a clinical problem.

'It has already gone too far for compromise. Syria is in

the land. Through the Groups she controls, Iran intrigues to impose Fundamentalism. That creed seeks always to contain men within strictly defined boundaries, to hold them slave-obedient to old-fashioned laws probably suited to the age they were promulgated in but – not for our times. In God's name, not for our times! The Groups that are supported by the Ayatollahs – the FFP the most formidable of them – have their ethos rooted in the fundamentalist interpretation of the Quran: should they emerge as victors here, then Lebanon is finished as a modern state. Fundamentalists look only backwards, to the past. They desire only stagnation and they have to be stopped. *Destroyed!*'

Appalled, she stated the obvious conclusion to what he had said:

'And AKAL to be the instrument of that destruction?'

'Surely –' But Soheil's concentration had been broken into by what he was seeing ouside the car; he was leaning forward over the wheel, peering ahead. 'That's the main road over there?' he asked. 'Turn right, and we're not far from Al Ain?'

'Correct.' She sat silent while he made the turn, intending then to bring the conversation back to Tagarid. But he spoke before her, easing into top gear, settling back into his seat.

'I fooled them,' he said suddenly. 'My God, I fooled them, I've *got away with it!*' Triumph unmistakable in his voice.

Puzzled but intrigued, she shook her head. 'Got away with what?'

'The FFP had me in their hands and *they let me go!*'

She perceived the boastful pride in him. 'You and seven others,' she pointed out.

'Ah, but I was *different* from those seven others.' He

flung it at her, delighting in his uniqueness. 'I'm the man the whole thing was about from the beginning!'

Sensing deep waters all at once opening at her feet:

'What *was* it "about" then?' she asked. 'Apart from the usual hostage-taking syndrome?'

He let it blossom in all its glory inside his own mind before he told her: driving without haste through the foothills of his Lebanon – peaceful and freedom-loving they looked in the slanting sunlight of afternoon, long slopes and fertile valleys – savouring the richness of his personal victory. Then:

'FFP seized the eight hostages in the hope of using them to pressure AKAL,' he said. 'Holding them, demanded from AKAL, as the price of their release, the identity of the AKAL leader responsible for the hit against Abu Hamad –'

'In effect, for the killing of his daughter and the injuring of his son.'

'Yes, that ... I myself was responsible,' he added quietly. And then self-admiration had him by the throat again: '*I am that man!*' he exulted. '*I* am the one Abu Hamad wanted above all others. And by a way-out chance, I fell into his grasp. I was there, at his mercy; but I outsmarted him and his interrogator. So *I go free; and now they'll never know what they lost.*'

'In AKAL, you have – executive powers?' Futile question; but it keeps it at bay, for a moment ...

He nodded; in his arrogance was barely aware of her except as the "receiver" of his confidences, of his triumph. 'Yes. I've been after Abu Hamad for nearly a year,' he said. Laughed, adding, 'Well, he's still there. But so am I. Soon I'll try again.'

Lois sat stunned. Soheil a terrorist. Plain truth out of his own mouth: he was not merely a 'supporter' of

AKAL as she had first assumed – with relief – when he was speaking of the threat Iran (among others) posed to the Lebanon; *he held a position within that Group which allowed him to order and organize terrorist action. A high position therefore.* Just as that AKAL man had informed Tagarid all those days ago. Assailed by dismay and horror:

'Will you tell Tagarid what you have told me?' she asked stiffly.

'That I'm with AKAL?'

'She's been told that already – though I don't think she believes it. No, I mean, will you tell her about this – of your status within the Group, that terrorism, killing, is part of your life? That you have influence, are one of the leaders –' The words hard to get out.

'No. Never ... But I wanted to, *tell you.* I needed to tell someone – some other person. Odd. It all seems more real to me now I've done that ... How did Tagarid find out I might be in AKAL?'

'They sent a man to see if she knew anything more than they did about your abduction. FFP were making trouble for her –'

'I remember my interrogators saying they were harassing you women ...'

Lois closed her eyes, turned away from him and fought to a standstill the hysteric laughter surging up inside her. "Harassing ... women"! In Britain that usually means men making unacceptable passes, fumbling you on trains, or calling out sexually degrading epithets – not planting car-bombs or tearing your home apart ...

Recovered, she asked coldly, 'So what about Tagarid? You intend to keep the truth from her? Just – go on as before?'

'She is still beautiful. She is my wife; and to my way of

thinking marriage is for ever. In my own fashion, I love her.'

'You have changed towards her. From the early years.'

'Other things claim me. They always will.'

'You say you won't tell her you're a – that you're actively involved with AKAL.' She paused for a moment, railing at herself: the word is *terrorist*, girl, why can't you use it to his face? But the answer came pat: because all this affects you too closely, that's why! Because you are afraid – not of him (not yet) but of the fact that he, your sister's husband, is one of that breed of men you have loathed and despised ever since you came to understand something of the insidious and destructive power of their dreadful brotherhood ...

Nevertheless, she could not bring herself to disown the euphemism she had employed; letting it stand, asked simply:

'*Why* aren't you going to tell her?'

They had reached the suburbs of the city and the streets were busy once again, packed with humanity. Soheil took his time to answer, muttering a curse at an aggressive driver once, his attention on other traffic and pedestrians. And when it finally came, his answer was brutally short:

'She wouldn't understand,' he said.

'*I* don't understand either!' Angrily, and the tide of her anger carrying her on now: '*Terrorism*, that's the name for those "other things" you say claim you –'

'Shut up!' He said it low and hard; went on swiftly: ' "Terrorism" is necessary to ensure that Lebanon does not fall to the forces of Evil, for terror tactics can only successfully be fought by the same methods –'

'All this to create a state within which *you* can pursue

your work?'

'Lebanon safe from the dead hand of Fundamentalism; people free to use their talents *in whatever
way they wish* for the benefit of their fellow-men: the end
justifies the means.' He said this quietly, out of the
self-centred certainty in him; he was not pleading his
cause to her, he was reciting his credo.

Lois found herself unable to argue with him. And in
that moment knew that from now on she would 'belong'
to Britain, not to Lebanon; that to live 'half-and-half'
smacked of opportunism, was but a selfish taking from
each side of the things she desired, saw as good (for
herself!) – while leaving the horrors for other people to
deal with ... To live like that had surely to be a basic
dishonesty which in the end would leave one in a limbo
of one's own making ...

'I wish you hadn't told me,' she said at last, speaking
almost casually into the silence that had developed
beween them. She felt very distant from him, and sad:
as if he were a total stranger. The entity that had existed
in her mind as "Tagarid-and-Soheil" had self-
destructed ... To her surprise she heard him laugh; and
attended to his answer then.

'Lois, I'm not a modest man,' he said. 'Surely you
know that much of me by this time. I wanted – needed,
perhaps, after the tight restraint I'd imposed on myself
during the days of my imprisonment – to let myself go,
to make one tremendous *shout*, as it were, just once, in
praise of my own skill and courage and intelligence.' He
laughed again, mocking – yet believing in – his own last
words. 'It's a wonderful feeling,' he cried, lifting his
hands for a moment off the wheel. 'To know *you have
won*. The enemy, defeated: beaten, on his own ground,
by you, fighting against all of them, alone.'

Thirteen

That evening Abu Hamad and Ramadan Saad sat out their time of waiting in one of the committee rooms inside an FFP stronghold ... The surveillance on the Fanous apartment was still being maintained. The two (picked) men on duty there were in plain clothes but fully armed. Both were totally familiar with the Shams apartment block and its environs, knew by sight all those who usually frequented it – having been in position outside, on and off, for many days – and on this occasion, had been comprehensively briefed. Their orders were to continue surveillance, reporting in immediately, by telephone, any attempt to leave the building by either Soheil Fanous or his wife, or his wife's sister Lois Everard; to monitor all arrivals – heading either for the Fanous apartment or the only other occupied flat in the block – and report in on anyone 'suspicious' or unknown to them; to keep watch for the (possible) infiltration of AKAL gunmen into the area; lastly, to take note of the time of arrival of Abu Hamad himself, together with one companion, and his entry into the building, after which they were to hold themselves in a state of maximum readiness. If, during the next couple of hours, the situation outside the block 'changed' in any way; or if, by the end of that time, neither Abu Hamad nor his aide had reappeared, they were to act on their own initiative, call up reinforcements (stationed nearby) and storm the apartment, apprehending and taking into custody any non-FFP personnel they found there ...

Saad arrived at the rendezvous first, at 6.30; Abu Hamad five minutes later. Both men were wearing fatigues; hand weapons they would pick up as they left on their mission, a holstered pistol each, silencers carried separately to be fitted later, just before they entered the apartment; and in their Mercedes, two automatic rifles had been left ready for use in case of need.

'Nothing yet?' Saad got to his feet as Abu Hamad took his seat at the table.

'Shouldn't be long now.' Abu Hamad poured himself coffee from the pot standing on the electric heating-tray in front of him. 'Fanous and the woman went in at three-thirty, confirmation to the desk here. Provided he has followed instructions and phoned in to AKAL immediately on his arrival, the release of Mansoor, that is his safe delivery by the broker into FFP hands, should have been initiated within an hour. But that's a highly complex manoeuvre, bound to be with each side guarding against last-minute trickery. It will take time ...' He sipped coffee.

'The call confirming that Mansoor is restored to us – it will come to you here in this room? Or to the main desk?'

'Here.' He gestured towards the telephone on the sideboard. As he did so his eyes fell on the coffee-pot. 'Take coffee for yourself,' he invited.

Saad did so. As he sat down again in his place, facing Abu Hamad across the polished wood of the table:

'When he learns of it, Mansoor will not approve of this action of ours tonight,' he observed quietly.

'For the public record, he will register disapproval. Naturally. But I have already secured agreement – in principle – to my right to vengeance.'

'From?'

'The hawk among Mansoor's three top advisers. Inflamed by what he sees as AKAL's "victory" in this affair – for their abduction effectively neutralized our own initiative – he is well-pleased, privately, at the prospect of my strike against them. This approval will be passed swiftly along the internal communications of our organization *at the executive level*. Which is the only level that interests me –'

'Or holds any power over you within the Group.' Saad nodded.

'Right. So the safeguards to my position are firmly in place.' Abu Hamad leaned his elbows on the table. His voice deepened as he brooded on the coming confrontation. 'Fanous defeated his interrogator. Soon now, he will face me; and though it is possible he will defeat me, also, in the matter of the naming of the man I hold responsible for the death of Hessa, yet I will have some part of my revenge this night.'

'The girl –' But at that moment the phone rang, and Saad broke off as Abu Hamad got to his feet and crossed to it swiftly.

He took the call, listened for a minute; then said, 'We will move out immediately.' Replacing the receiver, he turned towards the door. 'Mansoor is in FFP hands,' he said. 'Time to go.'

Saad was already on his feet.

A quiet homecoming for Soheil Fanous. He took his wife

in his arms, held her tightly to him and did not notice
the lack of passion in her welcoming caresses, his mind
possessed still by the twin and glorious facts: first, he
was a free man; and second (that secondness designated
to it only because, of necessity, its reality depended on
the accomplishment of the first), he had pitted his wits
against the FFP and he had been the victor, had
succeeded in keeping from them the knowledge that *he
himself was the man they sought, the man their whole operation
had been aimed at flushing out.* Even as he kissed Tagarid,
he was remembering words spoken at his first
encounter with his interrogator; 'That man is marked
for death' the bastard had said ... And now (his arms
still round his wife) Soheil Fanous made answer to that
assertion, in the secret places of his own mind: 'That
man is now free, his true identity kept to himself against
all comers.'

Liliane greeted him, her great happiness in his safe
release piercing his self-regard (for he saw in the girl
material to be moulded by his own will, he was already
directing her towards medical studies and saw himself
as her mentor, perhaps in time her teacher).

'What were your biology results?' he demanded,
disengaging himself from her embrace, stepping back.

She laughed, holding back tears. 'Damn good. Oh yes,
damn good. You'll be pleased. Details later, when you've
settled in.'

He turned again to Tagarid. 'She swears too much.'
Then, 'I have to make a phone call,' he said. 'Report
myself returned home in one piece. After that, by God,
a bath ...'

... By seven o'clock they were all in the lounge, with
the second bottle of champagne just begun. Tagarid
beautiful in severely styled rose brocade, recounting an

amusing anecdote from her work of the previous day, an ID check she had driven inland to make but then the 'man' she had sought turning out in fact to be a woman, the mistake originating in the papers she had been working from. Soheil at ease in an armchair, cream silk shirt and dark slacks, in truth only half-listening to her but his eyes on her face, the smile waiting ready for its entrance cue. Liliane in jeans and a white muslin overblouse lightly ruffled at wrists and neck; she was sitting on the floor, leaning one arm on the edge of a large circular pouffe, watching Tagarid with love. And Lois on the sofa, the bottle of champagne at her side in its ice-bucket (Soheil forbidden to do any 'work' whatsoever that evening – a diktat he had accepted without argument); but she had heard Tagarid's story before, and soon got quietly to her feet and went out, made her way along the corridor to the kitchen: the duck needed basting, and besides Liliane had eaten all the cashew nuts already and more were needed ...

As she walked back, her heels clicking on the tiled floor, a porcelain dish of nuts in her hand, she was wondering whether or not Tagarid would make love with Soheil that night. The two of them seemed to her to be each aware of personal separateness from the other, in spite of the welcoming hugs and emotional words – those, such as you would accord to any close *friend* in like circumstances, surely, they were not the prerogative of lovers? And would Tagarid now carry through her earlier intention, to leave him and create a life of her own, in the States? –

Opening the door into the lounge, she found herself face to face with a man holding a gun. A total stranger, his weapon pointed at her chest. Silencer fitted.

'Come inside,' he ordered in Arabic, edging a little

aside to allow her to do so.

Keeping her eyes on the gun she went into the lounge. He pushed the door shut behind her with his foot. As it slammed, she started, the dish in her hand tilted and cashew nuts cascaded down onto the carpet but she didn't notice, lifting her eyes to his.

'Stand quite still where you are.' His voice almost conversational in tone. 'Now look round at the others, carefully, so that you understand the situation in here.'

She found it difficult to take her eyes off the man, and his gun. But managed it, jerking her head round so that the whole of the lounge was in her view. Saw: a tableau, and everyone and everything in it perceived in sharp focus. Contained within the softly-lit elegance of the familiar room: facing her, Tagarid, risen from the chair she had been sitting in; Soheil, standing a few yards to the left of his wife, his arms at his sides; Liliane unmoved, frozen into her pose on the floor, leaning on the pouffe; and all three of them staring as though mesmerized at the second stranger in the room, the man off to her right, a burly grey-haired man and the gun in his hand levelled at Soheil. Silencer on that gun, also –

'Now walk across the room towards your sister, until I tell you to stop.' The voice of her "possessor" more menacing now. 'Do it slowly. Drop that dish you're holding and keep your hands clear of your body all the time.'

Lois looked down at the dish, surprised that she still had it. Then relayed a command from brain to fingers and a split second later saw the flowered porcelain fall to the floor. Carpet there, it did not break, she noticed; but what a mess roast cashews made –

'Move!'

She obeyed, step by measured step, until:

'Stop!' he ordered. 'Now stand right there and keep still. Any trouble from you and I shoot the girl in the stomach. Her first, then you.'

Lois took stock of her place in the tableau: to Soheil's left, about three yards separating them ... And the gun of the grey-haired man trained on Soheil but dominating Tagarid as well through that threat ... She remembered then that – like many people in Beirut – Soheil kept a loaded automatic in the house, it was in the top drawer in the tallboy in the master bedroom. But dismissed that hope almost instantly, the master bedroom was off along the corridor, no chance –

'Now we have the four of you secure, I will come to the point of our visit.' The grey-haired man addressed himself exclusively to Soheil; and stepped a little closer to him as he spoke. (Lois saw his face more clearly then: strong-featured, with a chilling ruthlessness lined into it; and the eyes bleak.) 'You know who I am.' His voice made it a positive statement.

'I do not.' Soheil met his eyes blandly, only too well aware of the identity of his questioner and counselling himself to proceed with extreme care in dealing with him.

'That is surely a lie.' But it had angered him. 'I'm stronger meat than that interrogator of yours, Fanous,' he said. 'I am Abu Hamad.'

'I know *of* you, yes. Who in Beirut doesn't! FFP Group, and highly placed –'

'As you are placed within AKAL, I think. But we will not waste time in sparring together, in trading insults and hatreds. I want from you the name of the man responsible for the attack on my car, two weeks ago, during which my daughter was killed. I have no score to settle with you personally; all I desire is one death, in payment for hers.'

'I don't have the information you seek.'

'But to save – you and yours – tonight you can telephone someone within AKAL who is in a position to name names. If you are what I think you are, such a man would give you the name for the asking if approached skilfully: he would see no reason to refuse.'

'I don't have contacts that high within the hierarchy.'

'No? They went to a great deal of trouble to get you set free.'

'I was merely one of eight men. As you must know yourself, a Group is tender of the morale of its members, and of its public standing: should it remain passive when eight of its people are taken hostage, both suffer. There is loss of prestige –'

A peremptory gesture with the gun. 'Enough! You mince words. I have stated what I want from you. Before you persist further in your denials, let me make clear the choices open to you here, now. They are simple. Either you provide me with that name; or, that girl' – with his free hand he pointed to Liliane – 'dies. And she dies the way Hessa died.'

Lois stiffened; held herself still. Her eyes darted to Tagarid's face: she read horror and panic there and glanced at Liliane. Saw a slight shudder pass through the girl's body and then the whole of her frozen, her eyes looking up sidelong at Abu Hamad and her gaze fixed on him with dread.

'You can't – ' Lois began but words dried in her mouth as her "guard" snapped out,

'Be silent or I shoot you first!'

Soheil moved restlessly, shifting his weight from one foot to the other. He frowned and shook his head.

Finally:

'But I *cannot* tell you what I do not know –'

'Use the phone and find out. *Find out!*'

Soheil gestured hopelessness, the open palms of his hands going out towards Abu Hamad in entreaty.

'I swear to God, I know of no-one who might tell me!' he protested. 'And Liliane, please – she's done nothing to you! Nothing to hurt you –'

'She hurts me by being alive when Hessa is dead.' Abu Hamad's voice had gone hard and flat; narrowed and unblinking, his eyes bored into those of Soheil Fanous (who saw in them that without any possibility of doubt this man would have himself a death; one way or the other he would have himself a death – and that *soon now*). 'Are you going to give me, or find out for me, that name?' he demanded. 'I ask you for the last time, understand.'

'I do not know the name you want, and I have no way of finding out. You must do as you will.' As he spoke, Soheil heard Lois catch her breath, and instantly recalled: *she knew the truth*. His thoughts ran wild: no, she cannot, dare not – not to *me* – she will not, tell. *Or will she?* So – jump her, throttle the life out of her, *stop her* – but Abu Hamad's gun moved fractionally, he flinched, and –

'*He's lying!*' Lois' voice break-point shrill. 'It was *him! He* organized that ambush! *He's* the man you seek!'

'*Bitch!*' Cold, hating; and Soheil's final word.

'Saad, cover Fanous, kill him if any of them make a move.' Abu Hamad snapped out the order; saw it obeyed and then walked over to Lois and stared her in the eyes. '*Fanous*, the originator and controller of that mission? That is what you are saying?' he asked softly.

Looking into his face, she found it surprisingly easy to go on with what she had started: they were two of a kind, he and Soheil; killers both, so it was right that *between them* should be the killing that was assuredly to come now.

'Yes!' she said.

'How do you know?'

'He told me himself. At two this afternoon I picked him up –'

'I know all that. Stick to the point.'

'As we drove back here he boasted to me of how he had fooled the FFP interrogator. He himself was the man you wanted, he said, the man the FFP were looking for. And you'd had him in your power but he'd outwitted you. Defeated you.'

For a long moment Abu Hamad searched her eyes. What she saw in his, intimidated her: she recognized her own fear and was not ashamed of it. Nor of the decision she had made, and implemented.

Abruptly, Abu Hamad gave her a brief nod; then turned and stepped across to Soheil, taking care not to cross Saad's line of fire. Halting close to him, levelled his weapon once more, at the revealed enemy.

'Watch the wife,' he instructed Saad. 'Keep her covered from now on. The girl won't cause trouble, nor will the sister. If Tagarid Fanous does, act as you think best. Kill her only if necessary; as you know I have no quarrel with her.'

In silence then, he stared hungrily into the face of Soheil Fanous (who gave him look for look but was dominated by the gun). At last:

'Yes,' he said. Then grief and fury gathered in his face. 'I would like to take you out into the hills.' His voice quiet but the more grim for that. 'Kill you bit by bit, enjoying it. But there's no justice in that, and I believe justice should be observed in these affairs. Death by the gun to be paid for in the same coin … There were three bullets in Hessa's body; shoulder, neck, and right eye –'

Tagarid screamed. Saad smacked her savagely across the temple with the barrel of his gun and she fell; lay sprawled on the floor, mouth gaping, eyes closed.

The weapon in Abu Hamad's hand unwavering. 'How long will she be unconscious?' he asked.

Saad knelt beside her, lifted an eyelid.

'Long enough,' he said.

'Then take the other two out of here. Get them into the hall. Keep them there until I come out.'

Menaced and driven by Saad's gun, moving with that slow drugged deliberation imposed by nightmare horror, Liliane dragged herself to her feet and stumbled towards the door. Lois followed. Neither of them looked at Soheil Fanous. (He has spoken no word since I 'named' him, Lois thought. Betrayal cuts the ground from beneath one's feet, I suppose ... Betrayal: ugly word. But my silence would have been a betrayal also; and better betray the guilty than the innocent ... Yes, it helps to think abstractions, doesn't it, keeps your mind off other things –)

Reaching the doorway, she heard the soft *phht!* of the first shot. Jerked round to look – and Soheil was already on his knees, blood pouring from his throat –

Saad gave her a violent push on the shoulder and she half-fell forward into the hall. Heard the door slam shut behind her.

Fourteen

In the hall, under threat of Ramadan's gun, Lois waited – Liliane beside her, weeping, moaning quietly to herself. The closed door sheltered them from the lounge, from Soheil, from Tagarid –

It opened. Leaving it ajar, Abu Hamad came out into the hall. Head down, he was unscrewing the silencer from his weapon; the task was the work of a few moments only and when it was done he dropped it into the pocket of his jacket. As he did so his eyes came up; to her's.

'Probably unwise for you to go back in there,' he said. 'We'll take you any place you want, friends, a hotel –'

'He is dead?' Thinking: this man looks satiate. No other word for it, *satiate*.

Abu Hamad nodded. 'The wife's still unconscious but when she comes round I don't imagine you'll find her friendly to you. This girl here, okay. But you' – He paused, an odd expression (a sort of respect, was it, Lois wondered? My God, who wants respect from a terrorist?) on his face. 'You, I imagine, she will hate for the rest of her life.'

'I can't leave her alone to deal with – that.' Curious, to be able to stand here and talk to him like this; we are skating over the top of very deep waters yet in some queer way I feel *he understands*. Surprisingly, understands many things –

'She can contact AKAL. They will handle it.' He smiled, mocking (but mocking himself as well as AKAL?). 'With the swift efficiency that comes of long practice,' he added.

'I'm her *sister*.' (It has a hollow sound, though, doesn't it? "Sister". Sister who made death for her sister's husband – *chose* to do that. For however much one explains, in the final analysis that is how it stood: choice did exist.)

Abu Hamad's eyes inquisitive. 'Why did you finger him for us?' he asked.

Silent, she stared at him, trembling now. He and Soheil: brothers of the heart. *Brothers* …

'Out of the anger in me,' she said.

He turned away.

'Let's go,' he said to Saad, moving briskly towards the outer door. He made no further reference to his offer to take Lois out of that place. (So he *does* understand, she thought dully; *but he allows that understanding to affect nothing in his way of life*). Then the two strangers left the apartment of Soheil and Tagarid Fanous as they had arrived in it, without hurry, carrying hand-guns and by the front door.

When the door had closed behind them, she shuddered, and leaned for a few seconds against the wall. Then, with a tremendous effort, gathered together her resolve and turned to Liliane who was squatting now, head in hands, beside a glass-fronted cabinet displaying porcelain figurines.

'You'll help me?' she asked her.

The girl nodded; stood up shakily, rubbing her eyes, not looking at her. 'Tell me, what to do. How we, deal with what's in there.'

'We carry Tagarid into the bedroom, put her under the duvet. You stay with her. When she comes to, make her take two or three sleeping tablets, tell her everything's being dealt with –'

'But – if she asks about Soheil?'

'Say he's wounded. That the doctor's with him, so she must keep away for the time being.'

'Lies –'

'They can help sometimes. If you're willing to take to yourself the blame, the sin of telling them.'

'And – you? What are you going to do? About his, body?'

'There is a number an AKAL man left with Tagarid, a week ago. I shall ring it, tell them what's happened – no lies – and ask for their help … Are you ready now? Shall we do it?'

Liliane was already at the lounge door. 'Let's get her out of there before she comes round, and sees,' she said, going through.

… Tagarid still unconscious, when they pulled the duvet up over her chest. And, a little later, AKAL indeed demonstrating the swift efficiency Abu Hamad had predicted of them. They even had a doctor with them, who made sure that Tagarid was all right.

Fifteen

Lois came up the deep-end steps of the pool, pulled off her swimming-cap and shook out her hair. Strolled through sunlight – this area of the Dolphin Club deserted except for Tagarid and herself, for it was barely nine-thirty a.m. – back to her lounger beneath the awning. Picked up her towel and smoothed it desultorily over her arms, shoulders.

'You should go in,' she said to her sister. 'Lovely and cool.'

'Later, maybe.' Tagarid looked up from her sunbed. 'I'm glad you persuaded me to come,' she went on. 'To get – out …'

A week had passed since the revenge killing of Soheil Fanous: its days full, exhaustingly nerve-stretchingly full of people who had to be met, of things that had to be done. During its passage, Lois and Tagarid had progressed from a deliberate distancing of one from the other – no accusations voiced, but each working her way slowly free of the horrors keeping them apart – to a closeness balmed with a fresh mutual understanding, and acceptance of, the essential *difference* of the other.

'The first of June tomorrow.' Lois sat down, leaned back in her lounger. 'Leila's asked me to stay on till the end of term,' she said.

'That would be mid-July, wouldn't it ... Will you?'

'I don't know. I want you to make up your mind first.' Strange that it's not difficult to talk about it here, when at home the words stuck in my throat whenever I tried to say them. 'Are you going to leave here and go to the States? Make yourself a life there, as you planned to do before all this began?' That's what I found myself unable to ask before – I wonder was it out of respect for Tagarid's grief, or simply because I was afraid of what her answer might be? Well, it's asked now.

The answer came much more quickly than she had expected, and was definite, unequivocal.

'I'm staying here,' Tagarid said. 'Beirut is my place and I'm not leaving it. Too many people have left this country over the years – abandoned it – and very few have come back. But there's still many here, the majority, who loathe the stranglehold the Groups have on us. The politics of terrorism ...'

Lois turned and looked at her. She was sitting up now, legs drawn up in front of her, chin on knees: staring out at the blue water of the pool, her face intent, a new and resolute commitment in her eyes.

'I've no idea how to go about breaking that grip,' she went on. 'But if we don't the Lebanon will very soon become a wasteland. Maybe it's already too late. But there *are* organizations, individuals, working undercover to oppose those within the Groups who seek to dictate to us by terror. I want to play a part in *that* now – however menial – even if in the end it means I lose everything.'

'But how – how will you ever make contact?'

'I thought I'd go and see Uncle Jules, up at Byblos – I haven't seen him in years. He'll advise me, tell me what I can do.'

Lois lay back.

'I wish you'd told me all this before! Talked to me –'

'I'm glad I didn't. I had to reach the decision on my own – no, not on my own, it wasn't like that, I got to where I'm at by thinking about Soheil. I loved him; and when – after he was dead – I thought about him and what he was doing, it seemed to me he'd allowed himself to be drawn into terrorism by intellectual argument *and then tied into it*. Like a person is tied into a strait-jacket: terrorism a mental strait-jacket you can't win free of by yourself once you're in it ... Get "into" terrorism, and you'll only ever get out if someone outside, in the *real* world, reaches in and cuts a knot or two for you ...'

She lifted her head and faced her sister. 'I'd have liked to have done that for Soheil,' she said quietly. 'I see now that I should have made myself known to him, much more than I did. Not drawn away from him, hiding my hurt pride that my lover no longer sought me with the same covetous delight.' Turning away, she let a silence gather; and during it, herself moved away from the man she had once known.

'Well,' she said then. 'Will you stay on here as Leila asked you to?'

'May I?' Phrasing it thus, asked her sister's pardon for – many things.

Perceiving that: '*I want you to*,' Tagarid said.

Suddenly happy, Lois stretched her arms above her head, breathed in deeply; and then put her head back, closed her eyes and felt the sunshine warm on her eyelids.

'Thank you,' she said. Went on after a moment, thoughtfully, her eyes still shut. 'It's good at the school,' she said. 'Contrasts ... Beirut itself, the city, everywhere you go you feel suspicion and fear in people. The streets themselves seem haunted by a sort of threatening violence lying in wait for – *you*, perhaps. Any time, you'll be one of those passing by as some car-bomb explodes, oh, it's not you they're after but it's you they'll "get" all the same. Tough luck ...'

'And at the school?'

'A *good* feel. Smiles, good-humour, friendship; lots of joie de vivre – a bit too much sometimes, but the spirit of it's great. Oh I know a lot of the cheerfulness is a "front", a carefully maintained "front" – they know better than I possibly can the fear that's killing the city, squeezing the life out of it. But it's brave, isn't it? They *have to do it* in order to survive, to show to the world – and therefore themselves keep hold of, believe in – their *other* faces, yes, I understand that. Nevertheless, it's great bravery they have. I admire it very much.'

'Leila will be pleased you're staying. You'll tell her this morning, when you go in at eleven?'

'I will. And I'd better be on my way now or I'll be late –'

'Don't forget strawberries for tonight ...'

Lois changed into blouse and skirt, deposited her bag of swimming-gear at reception for her sister to collect and take home with her when she left the 'Dolphin', and took a taxi to Leila's Academy. 'Don't forget straw-berries': the words, floating into her mind as she was driven through the city, reminded her of Salaam. Energetic, homely Salaam, who had not come near the apartment since the day Soheil had been 'executed'; and of whom Tagarid had since told her a little more: a peasant girl from a village outside Damascus; seduced by 'a soldier' and the illegitimate son ten years old by this time, being brought up by her parents on the money she sent back to Syria ...

'Women like that are so easy to use. "Give us the keys to that apartment or you'll get no more money out of here for the rest of your life." Or, "Give, or your son will die." Or maybe even "Give, or *you* will die." '. Tagarid's words, those, the evening she came back from calling at Salaam's lodgings, having found there the cleared-out room up for hire and a stony-faced "concierge" who denied all knowledge of a forwarding address. 'Create a climate of fear, informed fear; then provided you can maintain it and enforce it, *in the end you will win.*' Tagarid's expression as she said that, it hurt me …

In the staffroom at one o'clock, morning classes ended, Geraldine came across to speak to her.

'Nizar brought news of Fahal Rizik last night,' she said. 'You asked me to see if he could find out why Fahal hasn't been in class for the last week.'

Lois busied herself putting textbooks into her locker: doing that, need not face the other girl.

'Good of him,' she said. 'I hope Fahal's all right?'

'Apparently he's already left for Saudi.'

'That job he'd been offered, I suppose.' Don't overdo the casualness, girl.

'Yes, must have been. His visa finally came through, Nizar said, and Fahal flew out the day after –' She checked herself, found a different time-link: 'Last Wednesday that was, you were absent yourself both the Tuesday and Wednesday, remember?'

Oh yes, I do remember. Put the exercise books inside. Close the locker. And look at her now, it will seem odd if you don't.

'I'm glad for him,' Lois said, picking up her shoulder-bag from the table. 'Maybe he wrote –'

'If not from here, he'll probably write you when he's settled in … Can I give you a lift?'

Lois refused the offer, preferring to walk. Then as she came into the entrance hall, Naji, the receptionist, called out her name. As she walked towards him across the parquet floor she saw he had an envelope in his hand; he was holding it out to her.

Fahal! His name inside her head and she quickened her pace. It's a note from Fahal, he hasn't gone out of my life leaving no word. And she took the envelope, smiling. It was quite heavy in her hand: one of those brown padded covers you buy when you want to give some protection to whatever it is you want to enclose within it. He has left me something to remember him by, she thought. But then she saw that the writing on it was in a hand unknown to her, not his.

Walking to the front door she went out into the courtyard where lilac and jasmine were flowering. No-one else around.

Standing, opened the package. Tipped the slit end of it up over her cupped hand: thick gold links spilled out into her palm; and within the pooled gold lay her scarab of polished dark green malachite. No note accompanied it.